School Stories
for Eight Year Olds

Helen Paiba is known as one of the most committed, knowledgeable and acclaimed children's booksellers in Britain. For more than twenty years she owned and ran the Children's Bookshop in Muswell Hill, London, which under her guidance gained a superb reputation for its range of children's books and for the advice available to its customers.

Helen was involved with the Booksellers Association for many years and served on both its Children's Bookselling Group and the Trade Practices Committee. In 1995 she was given honorary life membership of the Booksellers Association of Great Britain and Ireland in recognition of her outstanding services to the association and to the book trade. In the same year the Children's Book Circle (sponsored by Books for Children) honoured her with the Eleanor Farjeon Award, given for distinguished service to the world of children's books.

She retired in 1995 and now lives in London.

School

STORIES

for Eight Year Olds

COMPILED BY HELEN PAIBA

ILLUSTRATED BY LYNNE CHAPMAN

MACMILLAN
CHILDREN'S BOOKS

First published 2001 by Macmillan Children's Books
a division of Pan Macmillan Limited
20 New Wharf Road, London N1 9RR
Basingstoke and Oxford
www.panmacmillan.com

Associated companies throughout the world

ISBN 0 330 48379 X

3 5 7 9 8 6 4 2

A CIP catalogue record for this book is available
from the British Library.

Typeset by SX Composing DTP, Rayleigh, Essex
Printed and bound in Great Britain by
Mackays of Chatham plc, Kent

Contents

Trouble with the Fiend

Sheila Lavelle

I'm not the only person Angela plays tricks on. She does it all the time, to everybody. Friends at school, my dad, her dad, Miss Menzies up the street, strange ladies in cafés, even teachers. And even our new teacher, Miss March, which takes some nerve, I can tell you.

Miss March is the games mistress and our class teacher as well. We all call her Quick March behind her back because she's just like a sergeant in the army. She's sort of square-shaped with short black hair and solid legs like tree trunks. She wears great thick spectacles like the bottoms of jam jars and she has a bellowing voice that you can hear from the other end of the playing field. And you should just hear the way she yells at us.

"You have sixty seconds to get changed, starting from . . . NOW!" she shouts, standing in the corridor between the boys' and the girls' changing rooms. And woe betide anybody who isn't in their shorts and T-shirts and plimsolls by the time she blows that horrible shrieky whistle she wears on a green ribbon round her neck.

I was walking to school one Monday morning and I hadn't called for Angela that day, partly because I was still sulking with her for blowing up my mum's airing cupboard and spoiling our best sheets, and partly because the postman had just given me a letter with a London postmark and I wanted to read it in peace.

The letter was from my Uncle Barrie who teaches at a London comprehensive school. And I got a very nice surprise when I opened it because there was a five pound note inside as well as a belated birthday card and one of his funny poems. I was having a good giggle at the poem when I heard Angela's voice behind me.

"Charlie," she called. "Wait for me."

I waited until she caught up with me. She was all out of breath from running and she looked so pleased to see me that I hadn't the heart to be cross with her any more. We linked arms and walked on together and I started to tell her Uncle Barrie's poem.

"There was a young lady called Vickers
Who rode on a pony to Twickers
She rode round the town
And when she got down . . ."

I stopped because I could see she wasn't listening.

"I've got something to tell you, Charlie," she said. "Only you must promise not to give the game away." She kept breaking out into chuckles and giving little skips in the air as we went along. "Do you promise? Cross your heart and hope to die?"

"You're up to something," I said sternly, stopping on the pavement and staring at her mischievous face. "Come on, Angela. What is it this time?"

"Wait till you see what's in my satchel," she said, giggling more than ever. "That Miss March is going to get the fright of her life." She started to tug at my arm. "Stop dawdling, Charlie. We have to get to school before she does."

We arrived at the school gates at twenty-five to nine and there was still hardly anybody about. We hung our blazers in the girls' cloakroom and then took our satchels along the corridor to the classroom. I hung mine on the back of my chair, but Angela went straight over to Miss March's desk and lifted the lid.

"Angela," I said, in a shocked voice. "What are you doing?" Nobody is ever allowed to open the teacher's desk, and Angela knows that perfectly well.

She ignored me completely and took a small cardboard box with a few holes punched in the sides out of her satchel.

"Come and meet Freddy," she said, grinning.

4

I moved forward cautiously, praying it wasn't a spider. Or a bat. I've got a thing about spiders and bats.

Angela took the lid off the box and out hopped a little green frog.

"Oh," I said, smiling with relief. "Isn't he sweet? Where did you get him?"

"He was hopping round the lawn when I got up this morning," said Angela. "I thought I would bring him for the nature lesson. But then I had a better idea. I'll leave him in

Miss March's desk and he'll hop out when she opens the lid and I bet she screams the place down."

I doubted that very much. Miss March is the sort of person who isn't frightened of anything. If she wrestled with a sabre-toothed tiger she would probably win.

"It'll take more than a frog to scare her," I said. "Anyway, I think it's cruel. That poor little thing needs to be out in the fresh air. I think you're mean and I'm not going to have anything to do with it."

Angela stuck her tongue out at me and her face went all sulky as I stalked off back to the playground with my nose in the air.

"Stuffy old spoilsport," she called after me. So I was surprised to see that she had got over her sulks by the time the bell went, and gave me a wink and a friendly smile as we all trooped in and took our places.

Miss March breezed in and rapped on her desk for silence. And I winced as I thought of that poor little frog sitting there wondering if the sky was falling on his head.

"Good morning, class," boomed Miss March. And we all got to our feet and stood to attention like soldiers.

"Good morning, Miss March," we chorused dutifully, and everybody sat down. Miss March stood in front of the class and treated us to one of her nastiest smiles.

"A nice little surprise for you this morning, Class Five," she said. "Desk inspection." Our desks are supposed to be kept tidy at all times but of course we forget and let them get in a bit of a muddle. Miss Bennet always used to give us ten minutes to tidy up before desk inspection, but not Miss March. She's too mean. Sometimes I think she only does these sudden checks so she can grab the odd Mars bar or tube of Smarties that we're not supposed to bring to school.

Anyway, a great groan went rippling round the room and one or two people quickly lifted their desk lids and tried a crafty tidy up. But this wasn't allowed.

"All desk lids CLOSED," bellowed Miss March, and we all sank timidly in our seats and wondered who she was going to pick on first.

And of course she picked Laurence Parker, whose dad is the managing director of a sweet factory, and whose pockets are always crammed full of toffees and chocolates and stuff.

"Laurence Parker, you can be first," said Miss March, striding through the desks towards where he and I sat together in the middle row. Laurence Parker went red and I heard him say a very rude swear word under his breath. Then I saw him quickly raise his desk lid an inch or two and slide his hand inside. And before I knew what was happening I found a big crackly cellophane packet being shoved into my lap.

I looked down and my heart nearly stopped beating. Lying on my navy blue school skirt was a whole half-pound bag of Parker's chocolate caramels. There was no time to shove them back because Miss March was already looming over us like a thunderstorm. I couldn't slip them into my desk as mine was sure to be the next one to get inspected. So I did the only thing I could think of. I scooped them up under my cardigan and held them against my ribs with my elbow, praying that Miss March wouldn't notice the bulge.

Laurence Parker's breath came out in a long whistle of relief. He opened his desk lid wide, looking smug as anything because the inside was as tidy as could be.

"Very good, Laurence," said Miss March. "I wish everyone could be as neat. Now let's have a look at yours, Charlotte Ellis."

I wasn't worried about my desk. I knew I'd given it a good clear-out last thing on Friday. So I got a nasty shock when I opened the lid and found, right in the middle, on top of my nicely arranged exercise books, a small cardboard box with air-holes punched in the sides.

"And what might this be?" enquired Miss March, pouncing on the box and waving it in the air.

"It's um . . . er . . . it's a box," I mumbled, turning pink and hunching my shoulders as

I felt the bag of sweets start to slip out from under my elbow.

"I can see that," snapped Miss March, and the whole class tittered. "But what's in it?"

"Nothing," I whispered, looking daggers at Angela, who was laughing up her sleeve. "It's empty."

"Well, we'll soon see," said Miss March. And she opened the box and peered in. Everybody else craned their heads to look, but they were all disappointed because there was nothing but a few damp leaves and tufts of grass.

"I am waiting for an explanation, Charlotte," said Miss March coldly. And I sat there not saying a word. I could hardly tell tales on my best friend, could I? Even if she had put the box in my desk to get me into trouble.

Miss March pressed her lips together in a grim line and handed me the box.

"Take that and put it on my desk," she said. "And you can stand in front of the class until you decide you have something to tell me."

I shuffled to my feet, feeling the slippery bag of sweets slide even further down inside my cardigan.

"And stand up straight," Miss March added impatiently. "You look like the hunchback of Notre Dame." And she got hold of me by the shoulders and gave me a good shake.

And of course that's when I finally lost my grip on the bag of sweets and it shot out of the bottom of my cardigan and clattered to the floor. Everybody laughed at my red face, and that spiteful Delilah Jones said, "Oooh, Charlie Ellis," as if I'd stolen the crown jewels.

Miss March snatched up the sweets in triumph and took them back to her desk. She banged hard on the lid for silence.

"That's quite enough, everybody," she said. "As for you, Charlotte Ellis, you will stay in at playtime. And I shall want a full explanation of your behaviour. Your sweets are, of course, confiscated." And I held my breath as she opened the lid of her desk.

Well, that poor little frog must have been half out of its wits with all the banging because as soon as the lid was open it gave a great leap straight into Miss March's face. And Miss March let out such a shriek and jumped about half a mile in the air as if it was a nest of rattlesnakes in there and not just one little frog, and it just goes to show that even the toughest of people are usually frightened of something.

Anyway, it wasn't Miss March I was worried about. I was feeling sorry for the poor little frog. He had fallen to the floor and was now attempting pathetic little flopping jumps along the skirting board, cringing from the din everybody was making.

I didn't really stop to think. I ran up to the front of the class and picked up the frog as gently as I could. I popped him back into his cool leafy box and put him safely away in my desk. But I soon wished I hadn't.

The bedlam suddenly quietened and I looked up. There was Miss March, charging towards me like a rhinoceros, her face purple with rage. And it kept going white and then red and then purple again, like the disco lights at my Auntie Fiona's wedding reception.

I won't tell you everything she said. But I can tell you that it took a long, long time. I had to stay in every playtime for a whole week, and I had to write out one hundred times "I must not bring sweets to school", and one hundred times "I must not play practical jokes on my teacher".

Laurence Parker was ever so grateful that I hadn't told on him and he was as nice as pie to me afterwards. He walked home with me from school and he went with me to set the little frog free in a cool, boggy patch of ground near the Abbotsbrook stream. And he shared a whole box of sugared almonds with me that he had hidden in his blazer pocket in the cloakroom.

And who should come following us along the road, smiling away as if nothing had happened, but Angela.

"Get lost, Angela Mitchell," I said, in my best stuck-up voice. "I'm fed up with you and all the trouble you get me into."

And this time I really meant it. For a little while, anyway.

The Ruined Minibus

Gillian Cross

"**L**ook!" Barny Gobbo's mouth fell open as he stared through the school gates and he nudged Clipper and Spag. "What's happening?"

"Get off, Gobbo!" Clipper pushed him away and rubbed her arm. "How can anyone as fat as you have such pointed elbows?"

"Never mind my elbows," said Barny. "There's something important going on. The whole school's down by the front door."

That made Spag and Clipper take a look for themselves. Before the bell, everyone was supposed to go up the outside steps to the playground on the school roof and wait there. But this morning no one had obeyed the rule.

15

They were all crowded into the small space in front of the school, pushing and chattering.

"What is it they're looking at?" Clipper craned her neck, trying to see. "The minibus? But that shouldn't be parked there today. We haven't got a match. What do you think, Spag?"

Spag gave a patient sigh. "How about going to find out, instead of standing here guessing? Or is that too daring for you two?"

"Too daring for *me*?" Clipper pulled a face at him and charged ahead of the other two, pushing her way towards the front of the crowd. When she was almost there, they saw her stop.

"Oh no!" she shouted. "*No!*"

Barny lumbered up behind her. "Well don't just gasp. Tell us—" Then he saw for himself.

The minibus was parked right in front of the school door, with a ring of chairs round it to keep people away. It was in a terrible state. The windows were broken, the seats and the tyres were slashed and someone had battered the front with a heavy stone. There was a huge dent in the middle of the bonnet and it would not close properly.

And everywhere there were slogans, in red and yellow and blue, spray-painted over the top and the back and the sides. Things like:

BENNETT SCHOOL IS BO-O-O-ORING
and
BOO-HOO WE'RE BENNETT BABIES
and
POOH! BENNETT PONGS!

"Wow!" Spag said softly. He took off his glasses and cleaned them, as if he couldn't quite believe what he was seeing. "Someone's really gone crazy."

"But who?" said Barny. "Who would have dared—?"

"Must have been someone pretty big." Spag looked thoughtfully at the enormous stone that had been used to smash the bonnet. "I couldn't lift that. Shouldn't think even my dad could."

"Oh, who *cares* who it was?" Clipper kicked angrily at the chair in front of her. "Whoever

17

did it, it's a disaster. How am I going to get the cricket team to all the away matches? Mr Fox *always* takes us in the minibus. And what about the Inter-Schools Athletics at the end of term?"

"Oh, the end of term's weeks away," Barny said airily. "The minibus is sure to be mended by then."

"Want to bet?" muttered Spag. He had been scribbling busily in his notebook and now he was frowning down at what he had written. "Look at all the things that need doing." He held the notebook out so that the others could see.

New windows (6)
New windscreen (1)
New seats (3)
New bonnet (1)
Re-spray (all over)
New tyres (4)

Barny stopped smiling. "It'll cost a fortune. We'll never be able to afford it."

"We've *got* to afford it!" Clipper clenched

her fists fiercely. "We ought to win the cricket and the athletics this year. We've *got* to be able to get to the events."

"Honestly, Clipper," said a smug voice from behind her. "Sport, sport, sport. That's all you ever think about." Soppy Elaine Potter tutted and shook her head so that her plaits swung round her face. "You're so selfish."

"We can't all be as thoughtful and considerate as you and Sharon," murmured Spag solemnly.

Elaine gave him a suspicious look. She could never tell when people were teasing her. "At least me and Sharon think about other things besides *sport*. What about the First Years' picnic? How are they going to have that without the minibus to ferry them there?"

"That's right." Sharon was just behind Elaine, as usual. "They do *love* playing in the woods and . . ."

". . . and now they won't be able to go . . ." said Elaine in her most soggy voice.

". . . they'll miss it . . ." said Sharon.

19

". . . they're going to be so miserable . . ."

". . . *poor* little things . . ."

Barny turned away in disgust, thinking how Elaine and Sharon always enjoyed disasters. Like ghouls. As he turned, he saw Jenny McGrew, Spotty's little sister in the First Year. She was staring at Elaine and Sharon with a horrified, unhappy expression on her face. Barny turned back.

"Shut up, you two!" he hissed. "Can't you see you're upsetting people?"

Elaine ignored him. "They'll be the *only* First Years that never went on a picnic," she said dramatically. "And next year it'll be too late and—"

That was the last straw for Jenny McGrew. Her face crumpled up and she gave a loud, miserable wail.

"*See*?" Barny said angrily. He turned his back on Elaine and Sharon and put an arm round Jenny. Lucky he was so good with little kids, he thought. "Cheer up, Jen. The minibus'll be ready for the picnic. I – I *promise*. We'll all get lots of money and . . ."

Jenny looked a bit more cheerful but, before she could say anything, Mrs Rumbelow stepped through the front door and stood glaring at all the children.

"And what are you doing here? You know perfectly well that you should be up in the playground. Go on. Now."

Mumbling and grumbling, the children began to crowd up the steps, looking over their shoulders at the minibus. Barny was one of the last to leave and as he followed Spag and Clipper up he was frowning.

"We've got to do something," he muttered. "What's a good way to get money quickly? Lots of money."

Spag patted him on the shoulder. "Don't give yourself brain-strain, Gobbo. I should wait until after assembly if I were you. The Head Mister's bound to say something about it."

He was right. When they all sat down after singing the hymn, the headmaster walked slowly to the front of the platform and stared down at them.

21

"Now," he said, "I'm going to talk about something very important. I'm sure you all passed the minibus as you came into school today. And I'm sure you all noticed what sort of state it's in."

He held up a hand to stop the whispers.

"No need to start saying how terrible it is. Of course it's terrible. Shocking. Someone broke into the garage last night and did all that damage. I *hope* it wasn't anyone from this school . . ."

There was a pause while he looked down and three hundred innocent faces looked up. Then he smiled sadly.

"No, I'm certain you're all as surprised and horrified as I am."

Clipper nodded, shuddering, and in front of her Soppy Elaine and Sharon made comfortable tutting noises.

"But finding out who did it is a job for the police," the headmaster went on. "*Our* job is to think about repairing the minibus. It's going to cost a lot of money, but if we don't do it, our sports teams will suffer. And – I'm sure

I don't need to remind you – the First Years
will have to miss their picnic."

Soppy Elaine turned round with a smug
grin and stuck out her tongue at Clipper.
From the other side of the hall came a loud
sniff. Jenny McGrew was crying again.

"There's no point in feeling sorry for
ourselves," the headmaster said severely.
"What we've got to do is raise money, as
quickly as we can. I want you all to go back to
your classrooms now and discuss ideas. By

lunch time tomorrow, I'll put up a list on the big noticeboard to show what everyone is doing, and things can start straight away."

A lot of people looked surprised and he said it again, firmly, to make sure that everyone understood.

"I want us to begin *at once*. If we're going to get the minibus ready for the picnic, we haven't got any time to waste. You can get your schemes going and then, at the end of the week we'll have a Grand Fair, on Saturday, and let the public in to try them. So your ideas had better be good."

He nodded briskly at them and then stepped back to show that the assembly was over. As the classes started to file out, Clipper nudged Barny, who was next to her.

"Ouch!" he hissed. "Don't know why you go on about *my* elbows. Yours are like spikes."

Clipper ignored him. "Look," she whispered, "we've got to think of something really good, the three of us. I'm not giving Soppy Elaine the chance of going round telling everyone I don't care about the First

Years. What are we going to do?"

"Yes, how about it, Gobbo?" Spag nudged him from the other side. "We need one of your Ideas."

"If you don't both stop prodding me," muttered Barny, "I'll be in hospital for the rest of term and you'll be raising money to bring me grapes. Why don't you just let me alone to think?"

As they walked out of the hall and along the corridor, he was racking his brains. He wanted something new. Something brilliant. And something that would make a lot of money. He hunted round his mind, like someone rummaging in a cupboard, but the cupboard was bare. On every side, people were chattering excitedly, working out schemes, but he didn't seem to have an idea in his head.

"Well?" said Clipper, the moment they sat down in the classroom. "What are we going to do?"

Barny frowned. "I haven't quite worked out—"

He didn't even know how he was going to end the sentence and he never found out. Mr Fox tapped on his desk with a ruler and looked round at them all.

"Right, everyone. Now, I can see that you're all bursting with fantastic, money-making ideas, so let's hear them. We'll use anything that's legal and possible."

Instantly, all over the room, hands went up and people began to call out.

"Sir!"

"Sir, sir!"

"I've got an idea, sir!"

Mr Fox put his hands over his ears. "One at a time! Yes, Elaine?"

Soppy Elaine stopped chewing her plaits and stood up. "Well," she said, taking a deep breath, "I've got a really *beautiful* doll. Her clothes are silk and her eyes open and close – at least, one of them does – and she *talks* and—"

"Elaine," Mr Fox said patiently, "I'm sure your doll is amazing. But how is it going to help us to raise money?"

"I was coming to that, sir." Soppy Elaine sounded hurt. "Me and Sharon are going to take her round the school and get people to pay five pence to guess her name. Then, after a week, we'll open up the envelope that has her real name in and give her to the person who guessed it. Of course, it'll mean I have to give up my doll, but I don't care if only the First Years can—"

"Yes, yes, Elaine," Mr Fox said. "We've all got the idea." Once Soppy Elaine really got going, it was very difficult to stop her. He turned and wrote on the blackboard.

Elaine and Sharon – NAME THE DOLL

As soon as he turned back, Spotty McGrew was on his feet. "I've got a *great* idea, sir. It'll be really fun and I've got a fantastic secret prize to give for it."

"All right." Mr Fox nodded. "What is it?"

Spotty beamed. "Skittles! I'm going to set up a skittle alley in the playground and at the end of a week the highest score with five balls will win the secret prize."

From all over the classroom, there were loud groans.

"Unfair!"

"We *know* who'll win that."

"No point in anyone else going in for it."

Mr Fox smiled. "If you want your competition to be a success, I think you'll have to ban Caroline from taking part. How about it, Caroline?"

"I don't care," Clipper shrugged. "I'm going to be too busy making money myself to worry about winning any skittles competition."

As Mr Fox turned away to write up Spotty's idea, she glared at Barny.

"Come on! What *are* we going to do?"

"Why has it always got to be me?" Barny said. He was annoyed because he still hadn't had an idea. "You can think too, can't you?"

"All right." Clipper gazed round at the classroom walls as though she expected an idea to pop out of the paintwork. "We could . . . we could . . ." Then she beamed. "We could have a sponsored high jump. Get people to pay a certain amount for each centimetre of our highest jump. Everyone would pay, just to have the chance of watching Spag."

Spag's high jumping was famous. Mr Fox said it was like seeing a giraffe ballet dancing.

But Barny shook his head. "Can't do that. After the last sponsored walk, my mum said she'd go mad if she saw another sponsor form this year. She said she'd come up to the school and complain. Herself. Personally."

"Oh." Clipper drooped. "Well, we can't do that, then." Mrs Gobbo on the rampage was worse than a herd of hungry elephants. "Well – er – how about knocking on doors and offering to do jobs for people?"

"I did that when I was in the Cubs," Spag said darkly. "I only ever visited one house. The old man there kept me working in his garden for four hours and then gave me five pence. And I was too stiff to do anything else for the rest of the week. We'll never make a lot of money like that."

Clipper frowned. "But we've got to think of *something*!"

She spoke more loudly than she meant to and Mr Fox looked across at her.

"Yes, Caroline? Have you got an idea you want to share with us?"

"Er – no, sir. Not quite."

Soppy Elaine and Sharon sniggered behind their hands.

"It's not *ready* yet," Clipper said fiercely. "Gobbo and Spag and I are planning something really brilliant, but it's got to be worked out. We'll tell you all about it tomorrow."

"Why did you have to say that?" grumbled Barny as they came out of school at the end of the day. "Now we've got to think of something that's twice as good as anyone else's idea. And we've got to have it all planned by tomorrow, if we don't want everyone to laugh at us."

Clipper screwed her fists up. "I had to say something. *You* saw Soppy Elaine and Sharon. You didn't expect me just to keep quiet and say nothing, did you?"

"Not without having your mouth sewn up,"

murmured Spag.

Clipper glared at him, but before she could say anything, a small, excited figure came running up.

"I'm the first!" Jenny McGrew said proudly. "I've made ten pence for the minibus before anyone else has even started."

Barny smiled down at her. "Well done. What did you do?"

"I made these buns when I went home at dinner time." Jenny shoved a grubby paper bag under his nose. "You'll buy some, won't you? They're only five pence each."

Barny peered into the bag. The buns were small and greyish, with burnt currants all over the top. "I – er—"

"Oh, *Gobbo*!" Jenny's bottom lip began to tremble.

"All right, all right." Barny felt in his pocket and pulled out three five pences. "I'll have one for each of us."

"Oh *thank* you!" Jenny pulled three buns out of the bag and dropped them into his hand. "I'm going to make some every day and

31

get lots and lots of money."

She skipped off happily. Clipper looked down at the buns and grinned. "It's going to be pretty expensive for you, Gobbo, if you have to buy three of those every day."

Barny shrugged, but Spag gave a gloomy nod. "That's right. That's the trouble with all the ideas everyone's had so far."

"What do you mean?" Barny held out his hand. "Here, have a bun."

Spag took one. "Well, all of them – Spotty's skittle alley, Soppy Elaine's doll, Jenny's buns – they're all meant to raise money from people at school, aren't they? And the school's not exactly crammed with million-aires. Even when we have the Grand Fair, probably only the parents of people at school will come."

Barny looked thoughtful. "You mean we ought to try to raise money from people outside the school?"

"That's right." Absent-mindedly, Spag bit into his bun. "We need – ouch, *Gobbo*! What's this bun made of? I nearly broke my tooth."

"Shouldn't have such feeble teeth, should you?" Barny munched away at his own bun. "They're quite all right as long as you don't mind the taste of burnt currants. Here, Clipper, have yours."

Clipper backed away, shaking her head. "No thanks. I've got to go to the dentist's anyway, tomorrow morning. I don't want to walk in with half my teeth missing."

Spag stared at her. "You – *what*?"

"I've got to go to the dentist first thing in the morning," Clipper said. "You know. *Dentist*. The one who sticks his head in your mouth."

"You mean," Spag said carefully, "that you've promised the class we'll come in tomorrow with a brilliant idea – *and you're not even going to be there*?"

"Oh." Clipper frowned. "Yes, I'd forgotten about that." Then she smiled again. "But it's bound to be OK. I mean, Gobbo's sure to have one of his Ideas by then. You've never gone twenty-four hours without one, have you, Gobbo?"

Barny thought for a moment and shook his head.

"Well then, what's the problem? You can tell Mr Fox before I get there, can't you?"

"But we won't have a chance to discuss it," Spag pointed out. "*You* won't know what the plan is until we've told everyone else."

"Oh, *that* doesn't matter." Clipper waved a hand. "We've *got* to raise money for the minibus, and I'll do whatever you two agree on."

Barny looked at her. "You'll do anything at all?"

"Anything."

"Barny Gobbo! Where have you got to?"

Barny was wandering round the scrapyard. He peered out from a forest of hatstands and saw his mother's red, angry face looking through the window.

"Er – I'm here."

Mrs Gobbo spluttered. "Oh you are, are you? And do you ever mean to go to school?"

"I'm waiting for Spag."

"Well, he's late. You can just stop waiting and start walking."

"But I can't just—"

"OUT!"

"Yes, Mum. OK, Mum. Bye, Mum." Hastily, Barny picked up his school bag and slouched out of the gate. But as soon as he was out of sight, he began to dawdle again.

He didn't feel like going to school at all. All night he had tossed and turned, until his arms and legs ached and his sheets were twisted like ropes. But – no Idea. And now his head felt as if it was stuffed with cotton wool and his brains had gone on strike.

In spite of walking as slowly as he could, he reached the corner at last – and saw what he had been dreading. Spag, bright-eyed and eager, came bounding along the pavement with his long, skinny legs flying out in all directions.

"Hello, Gobbo. Sorry I'm late."

"That's OK."

Spag came level with Barny and slowed down to walk beside him. "Well?" he said, after a minute or two.

"Well what?" muttered Barny.

"Well, what's the brilliant idea, of course. What are you and me and Clipper going to do about raising money?"

"I – er—" Barny hesitated. Was there really any point in saying he hadn't got an idea? After all, he might have an inspiration on the way to school. It would be a pity to upset Spag before he had to. "I've got a few more details to work out before I tell you."

Spag looked at him suspiciously. "Is it a good plan?"

"Of course it is! Sensational! Better than anyone else's."

"Hmmm." Spag looked at him again. Barny bent his head and pretended to be thinking hard, and the two of them walked on in silence.

But not for long. As they came round the next corner, a loud, rude voice yelled at them from the other side of the road.

"Well, well, look who's crawled out of the gutter. It's two of the babies from the

Bennett. Boo-hoo-hoo."

"Oh no!" Spag groaned softly. "Not Thrasher Dyson."

"Hear you had a bit of bad luck at your school," smirked Thrasher, sauntering across the road towards them. "Someone did your minibus over, did they? Boo-hoo-hoo. Must have made a change for you all. The Bennett's usually so bo-o-o-oring."

Barny looked at him. "You seem to know a lot about it."

"Me?" Thrasher raised his eyebrows and opened his mouth wide. "*Me*? You're not suggesting I had anything to do with it, are you? Why would I go slashing seats and ripping tyres and spray-painting rude messages? You hinting something, are you?"

Barny looked at Thrasher's flat, fierce face and the bulging muscles in his arms. "Er – no, of course I'm not."

"You'd better not be." Thrasher smirked again. "I'm OK, see. I was with my brother all the evening, wasn't I?"

"There's *two* of you?" Spag murmured.

Thrasher peered suspiciously at Spag. "You trying to be funny? 'Course I got a brother. Tiny. He's over there in the shop. Want me to fetch him out?"

"I don't think we'll bother," Spag said politely.

"We've got to go to school," added Barny.

Thrasher snorted. "Goo-goo! Little goody-goodies! What's so great about Boring Bennett that you can't wait to get there?"

"It's better than King's Road, anyway," Barny said. He was beginning to lose his temper. "We beat you at football, didn't we? *And* at cricket."

"Football!" Thrasher jeered. "Cricket! Who cares about them? They're games for little kids. We've got something better to do at King's Road."

"Oh yes?" said Barny. Spag was pulling at his sleeve to try and make him move on, but he wasn't going to slink off and let Thrasher think he'd won the argument. "What have you taken up now, then?"

"Swimming!" Thrasher looked triumphant.

"Me and Darren and Andy swam a hundred lengths between us last Friday. Bet no one at the Bennett could beat *that*."

"You know the Bennett doesn't do swimming—" Spag began, but Barny kicked his ankle to make him shut up. He wasn't going to let Thrasher get away with boasting like that.

"'Course we could," he said. "Me and Spag and Clipper can beat you any time you like. Can't we, Spag?"

"Well—" said Spag.

Barny kicked him again and whatever Spag had been going to say changed into a grunt. Thrasher looked from him to Barny and back again.

"You reckon?" he sneered. "Ha ha ha. Help me, someone, before I die of laughter."

Across the road, someone came out of the newspaper shop and Thrasher turned round and called to him.

"Here, Tiny! Here's a couple of kids that reckon they can swim further than me and Andy and Darren."

"You're joking! Want to swim a marathon, do they?" Thrasher's brother strolled across the road and stood staring down at Barny and Spag, grinning at their expressions as they took him in.

He was about six and a half feet tall, with shoulders like goalposts and a face as ferocious as Thrasher's but twice the size.

"My brother," said Thrasher.

Spag raised his eyebrows. "Your brother – Tiny?"

"Yes," said Tiny. "It's a joke, see. Funny."

He pushed Spag's shoulder with a fist the size of a football and Spag gave a feeble grin.

"So these weeds think they're champion swimmers, do they?" Tiny grinned wider. "What do they reckon then, Thrasher? Two of them against any two of you?"

Thrasher shook his head. "No, there's three of them as well. The third one's a girl."

"A *girl*?" Tiny opened his mouth and bellowed with laughter. It sounded like an explosion in a quarry. "One suet pudding, one beanpole and one girl? Now this I've got to see."

"Well, we'll have to talk about it some other time," Spag said quickly, pulling at Barny's sleeve. "Gobbo and I are going to be late for school."

"Hang on now. Can't hurt to wait a minute more," said Tiny. He put one vast hand on Spag's shoulder and one on Barny's. "I really fancy seeing this swimming marathon. Tell you what," – he grinned sideways at Thrasher – "we'll have a little bet on it. If you three

41

weaklings can swim further than Thrasher and his mates, I'll pay you each ten pounds. If not, you pay."

"A swimming marathon," said Spag, faintly. "I don't really think—"

"A *Swimathon*," thought Barny. And at that moment, something happened to him. The thing he had been waiting for since yesterday morning.

He had an Idea.

"OK," he said. "You're on."

"*Wha-at?*" Spag turned round and stared at him.

"We'll do it," Barny said. "Look, Spag, it's a great chance to raise money for the minibus."

"The *minibus*?" Tiny looked at Thrasher and they both smirked. "Yes, I heard you had a bit of trouble there. You babies at the Bennett dropped your dummies, did you, when you saw the ruins?"

"Fell out of their prams!" chortled Thrasher.

"Such *nasty*, *rude* messages all over it. And such a heavy stone that someone had used to smash the bonnet in!" Tiny flexed his enormous muscles and looked thoughtfully at them. "Now who could have done such a naughty, *naughty* thing?"

"Can't imagine," grinned Thrasher.

They went off into roars of laughter and Barny looked at the two of them. They weren't a pleasant sight, with their ugly faces and their short, stubbly hair, but he *wasn't* going to let them put him off.

"So it's fixed, is it?" he said stoutly. "We'll have a swimming competition a week today. At the swimming pool."

Thrasher nodded. "Half past six in the evening. And no cheating, mind. No putting different people in your team."

"But—" said Spag.

Barny kicked him again. "'Course we won't. Me and Spag and Clipper will all swim for our side. OK? And yours?"

"Me and Darren and Andy," Thrasher said.

"And if we win," Barny was determined to get it clear, "you pay us thirty pounds altogether."

"Sure, sure," said Tiny. "Wow, I'm really *scared* of losing the money."

He and Thrasher went off into more roars of laughter. Barny could still hear them as Spag dragged him away along the road.

"Here! Let go!" As soon as they were out of sight round the next corner, Barny pulled his arm free and rubbed it. "What are you up to, Spag? My shoulder's nearly dislocated."

"Pity your tongue's not dislocated," Spag said bitterly. "You idiot, Gobbo! You super, prize dumbhead! What did you think you were doing?"

"What's the matter?" Barny looked hurt. "You asked me to have an idea for raising money and I've had a brilliant one. We'll get thirty pounds altogether and we won't have to ask for a penny from the other kids at school."

"But we'll only get thirty pounds if we *win*!" Spag said despairingly, tugging his hair. "Even if we do win, I don't suppose it'll be easy making Thrasher and Tiny pay up. But what about if we *don't* win? We're going to have to pay *them* thirty pounds if we lose."

For a second Barny felt quite sick. Somehow he hadn't thought about that side of it. Then he tossed his head.

"Oh come on, Spag. Why should we lose? Thrasher thinks he can beat us easily because he's seen us play cricket and football and he knows you and me aren't exactly the stars of the team. Well, *you're* not, anyway."

Spag looked at him, but he didn't say anything.

"But I'm a very good swimmer," Barny went on. "I swam fifty lengths last month. And what about you?"

"I've done thirty-two, I think," said Spag, "but—"

"Well, there you are, then. Clipper only needs to do twenty or so to beat the King's Road lot and she's sure to be able to do that. She's probably better than both of us." Barny thought for a moment. "Well, better than you, anyway."

"Gobbo," Spag looked even more gloomy, "has it ever crossed your mind that—"

But he never got to the end of the sentence,

because just at that moment they both heard the clang of a bell, two streets away.

"We're late!" squawked Barny. "Come on!"

They raced up the road as fast as they could, but it was no use. By the time they panted up the stairs to the classroom, Mr Fox was just shutting the register.

"Well, Gobbo?" he said. "Well, James? What very important thing has stopped you getting here on time?"

"Er—" said Spag.

"We were making a plan," Barny interrupted. "To raise money for the minibus. We had to settle all the details before we could come."

"Really," said Mr Fox. "I hope it was worth being late for."

"Yes it was." Barny looked defiantly at Spag. "It's a really good plan and we're going to raise *thirty pounds* for the minibus. Me and Spag and Clipper, on our own."

People started to mutter and even Mr Fox looked surprised. But all he said was, "Well, tell me what it is, so that I can add it to the list."

"It's – er—" Barny thought quickly. "Well, it's a sort of sponsored swim, I suppose."

Mr Fox wrote on the board.

Barny
James   } SPONSORED SWIM
Caroline

Then he nodded. "Not a bad idea. You'll be able to take your sponsor forms round at the Grand Fair, won't you?" He put the chalk down and dusted off his hands before Barny could answer. "Right, then. Sharon can copy down our list of fund-raising ideas and take them to the headmaster's office. And the rest of us will do some work."

Clipper got to school at exactly ten o'clock. The whole class was doing Art, building huge models of robots out of eggboxes and cardboard tubes. As she walked through the door, Barny waved his arm at her.

"Hey! Clipper!"

"Gobbo!" said Mr Fox in a terrible voice.

"What are you doing?"

"I was only waving to Clipper, sir, because I wanted to tell her—"

"It's a pity you couldn't wave with an *empty* hand," said Mr Fox sadly. "Look around you, boy. Look what you've done."

Barny looked. "Oh," he said. "Oh dear." He had completely forgotten that he was holding the open glue-pot. There were huge splashes of glue all round him, on the floor, on the table and on the robot he and Spag were making.

"All right, Gobbo." Mr Fox looked patient. "Get a cloth and clear it up. Whatever you wanted to say to Caroline can perfectly well wait until break."

He sent Clipper over to the other side of the room, to help Spotty McGrew with his model, and watched Barny sternly. Every time Barny tried to signal to Clipper, to get her to look at their names on the blackboard, Mr Fox frowned and shook his head.

"Don't be so thick, Gobbo," hissed Spag. "If you don't stop doing that, Mr Fox'll keep you in at break and then you won't be able to talk to Clipper at all."

"But I just want her to know—"

"Oh, she'll know soon enough," Spag said. He didn't sound at all cheerful about it. "Now stick this eggbox underneath the other one. We need some more knobs on the control panel. *If* there's any glue left in your pot."

Barny sighed and took the eggbox. It was very difficult to concentrate on one thing when your mind was bursting with something else. He was really looking forward to telling Clipper about the swimming competition. She liked things to do with sport and she'd love the chance of beating Thrasher Dyson again. Perhaps Spag would appreciate the idea properly when he saw Clipper being enthusiastic. Barny looked across at her again and wished he could say just one word.

Then, ten minutes before break, Clipper caught sight of what was on the blackboard.

She was painting the leg of Spotty's robot with bright red paint and, as she moved round to get at the other side of it, she glanced up for a moment. Barny saw her read the words Mr Fox had written and he waited for her to look over at him and grin. But she didn't. She went on standing there, staring at the board, with her paintbrush dripping red paint all over the floor. Then Spotty nudged her and she bent down and started mopping up the paint with newspaper, before Mr Fox could see it.

Oh well, thought Barny. Only another ten minutes and then he could tell her properly.

But he wasn't prepared for what happened. The moment Mr Fox said they could go outside, Clipper shot across the room and grabbed Barny's arm.

"Right, Gobbo. Now tell me what's going on!"

"Ouch!" Barny pulled his arm away. Why did everyone always have to grab him in exactly the same place? "Well, it's brilliant. You see—"

Spag gave a quick warning cough, to tell them that Soppy Elaine and Sharon were standing a couple of feet away, ears flapping.

"Don't you think we ought to go upstairs and discuss this in the playground? Where we can be *private*."

Soppy Elaine sniffed and started talking loudly to show that she wasn't interested, but Clipper nodded.

"Yes," she said. "I think we're going to need to be really private."

Barny wondered why she sounded so serious, but he let himself be hurried upstairs and he stopped talking while they struggled across the playground to their special, secret place behind the chimneystacks.

It *was* a struggle too. Every yard or so, there was someone trying to get them to buy something or enter a competition. They had hardly got outside before Jenny McGrew was on top of them, waving a paper bag.

"Ginger buns today, Gobbo. I saved you some. Specially."

Barny sighed and dug in his pocket for some money. But the moment they escaped from Jenny, Spotty was waving at them and shouting.

"Here, Gobbo, come and have a go at the skittles. And you, Spag."

"They can't come yet!" Clipper shouted crossly. She pulled Barny and Spag away from the skittles and hurried them over towards the chimneystacks.

"Right," she said, as soon as they were sitting tucked away in their corner. "Now what's all this about a sponsored swim?"

"It's a brilliant idea," Barny said, before Spag could get a word in. "We won't need to pester anyone in the school for money and we'll raise thirty pounds for the minibus."

"*If* we win," Spag said. "Otherwise we'll have to *pay* thirty pounds. Somehow." He groaned and buried his face in his knees.

Clipper looked from one to the other. "But I don't understand," she said. "How do you know how much money we're going to raise? And where will it come from?"

"It's—" Barny wriggled. "Well, actually, it's not *really* a sponsored swim. More a sort of bet. The money's coming from Tiny Dyson."

"*Tiny* Dyson?" Clipper frowned.

"Thrasher's brother. His *big* brother." Spag raised his head for a moment, pulled a face and then doubled over again.

"And what have we got to do to win this — bet?" Clipper said in a small voice.

"Nothing difficult at all." Barny waved a podgy hand. "We've just got to swim further than Thrasher and two of his friends. That's about a hundred lengths, and I can do half of those by myself."

"And Spag?" Clipper said, so softly that she was almost whispering.

"Spag can do another thirty or so."

Clipper took a long, deep breath and then she yelled, at the top of her voice. "Gobbo, you fat porridgehead, why didn't you *ask* me before you landed us in the swimming pool with Thrasher and his brother?"

"But why did I need to ask you?" Barny said. "You told us you'd do *anything* to raise some money."

"But you wouldn't expect me to fly, would you?" Clipper said angrily.

Barny looked at her, and then at Spag, and then back at Clipper again. "What's flying got to do with it? That's quite different. You *can't* fly."

"*And I can't swim, either*!" shouted Clipper.

SCHOOL STORIES FOR RIGHT YEAR OLDS

The Christmas Party

George Layton

Our classroom looked smashing. Lots of silver tinsel and crêpe paper and lanterns. *We'd* made the lanterns, but Miss Taylor had bought the rest herself, out of her own money. Oh, only today and tomorrow and then we break up. Mind you, if school was like this all the time, I wouldn't be bothered about breaking up. Putting up Christmas decorations and playing games – much better than doing writing and spelling any day. I watched the snow coming down outside. Smashing! More sliding tomorrow. I love Christmas. I wish it was more than once a year.

Miss Taylor started tapping on the blackboard with a piece of chalk. Everybody was talking and she kept on tapping until the only person you could hear was Norbert Lightowler.

"Look, if I get a six and land on you, you get knocked off and I still get another go!"

The whole class was looking at him.

"Look, when Colin got a six, he landed on *me* and *he* got another . . .!"

Suddenly he realized that he was the only one talking and he started going red.

"Thank you, Norbert, I think we all know the rules of Ludo."

Miss Taylor can be really quite sarcastic sometimes. Everybody laughed. Even Miss Taylor smiled.

"Now, since it is getting so noisy, we're going to stop these games and do some work."

Everybody groaned and Tony and me booed – quietly so Miss Taylor couldn't hear. She hates people that boo. She says people who boo are cowards.

"Who is that booing?"

We must have been booing louder than we thought.

"Who is that booing?"

Miss Taylor looked at Tony. I looked at Tony. They both looked at me. I put my hand up.

"It was me, Miss."

Tony put his hand up.

"It was me an' all, Miss."

She looked at us.

"You both know what I think of booing, don't you?"

We nodded.

"Yes, Miss."

"Yes, Miss."

"Don't ever let me hear it again."

We shook our heads.

"No, Miss."

"No, Miss."

She turned to the class.

"Now, the work I have in mind is discussion work."

Everybody groaned again, except me and Tony.

"I thought we'd discuss tomorrow's Christmas party!"

We all cheered and Miss Taylor smiled. We have a Christmas party every year, the whole school together in the main hall. Each class has its own table and we all bring the food from home.

"Now, does everybody know what they're bringing from home for the party tomorrow?"

I knew. I was bringing a jelly. I put my hand up.

"I'm bringing a jelly, Miss!"

Everybody started shouting at once and Miss Taylor moved her hands about to calm us down.

"All right, all right, one at a time. Don't get excited. Jennifer Greenwood, what are you bringing?"

Jennifer Greenwood was sitting in the back row next to Valerie Burns. She wriggled her shoulders and rolled her head about and looked down. She always does that when she's asked a question. She's daft, is Jennifer Greenwood.

"C'mon, Jennifer, what are you bringing for tomorrow?"

She put her hand up.

"Please, Miss, I'm bringing a custard trifle, Miss."

Norbert Lightowler pulled his mouth into a funny shape and pretended to be sick.

"Ugh, I hate custard. I'm not gonna have any of that!"

Everybody laughed, except Miss Taylor.

"Well, Norbert, if I was Jennifer I wouldn't dream of giving you any. Right, Jennifer?"

Jennifer just rolled her head about and

giggled with Valerie Burns. Norbert was looking down at his desk.

"And, Norbert, what are you bringing tomorrow?"

"Polony sandwiches, Miss, my mum's making 'em, and a bottle of mixed pickles, Miss, homemade!"

Miss Taylor said that would be lovely, and carried on asking right round the class. Tony said that he was bringing a Christmas cake. I was bringing the jelly that my mum was going to make, and Colin Wilkinson was bringing some currant buns. Valerie Burns said that she was bringing some lemon curd tarts, and Freda Holdsworth called her a spiteful cat because *she* was buying the lemon curd tarts, and Valerie Burns *knew* she was bringing lemon curd tarts because she'd told her and she was a blooming copycat. Anyway Miss Taylor calmed her down by saying that it was a good job they were both bringing lemon curd tarts, because then there would be enough for everybody, and everybody would want one, wouldn't they? And she asked everybody who would want a lemon curd tart to put their hands up, and everybody put their hands up. Even I put my hand up and I hate lemon curd. Well, it *was* Christmas.

After everybody had told Miss Taylor what they were bringing, she said that there'd be enough for the whole school, never mind just our class, but we should remember that Christmas isn't just for eating and parties, and she asked Tony what the most important thing about Christmas is.

"Presents, Miss!"

"No, Tony, not presents. Christmas is when the baby Jesus was born, and that is the most important thing, and when you're all enjoying your presents and parties this year, you must all remember that. Will you all promise me?"

Everybody promised that they'd remember Jesus and then Miss Taylor started asking us all how we were going to spend Christmas. Freda Holdsworth said she was going to Bridlington on Christmas Eve to stay with her cousin, and on Christmas Eve they'd both put their stockings up for Father Christmas, but before they'd go to bed, they'd leave a glass of milk and some biscuits for him in case he was hungry. Norbert Lightowler said that that's daft because there's no such thing as Father Christmas. Some of the others agreed, but most of them said course there is. I just wasn't sure. What I can't understand is, that if there *is* a Father Christmas, how does he get round everybody in one night? I mean the presents must come from somewhere, but how can he do it all by himself? And Norbert said how can there be only *one* Father Christmas, when he'd seen *two* down in town in Baldwin Street and another outside the fish market, and Neville Bastowe said he'd seen one in Dickenson's. Well, what about the one my mum had taken me to see at the Co-op? He'd promised to bring me a racer.

"Please, Miss, there's one at the Co-op an' all. He's promised to bring me a racer."

And then Miss Taylor explained that all these others are Father Christmas's brothers and relations who help out because he's so busy and Freda Holdsworth said Miss Taylor was right, and Norbert said he'd never thought of that, but that Paul Hopwood, he's in 2B, had told him that Father Christmas is just his dad dressed up, and I said that that's daft and it couldn't be because Father Christmas comes to our house every year and I haven't got a dad, and Miss Taylor said that if those who didn't believe in Father Christmas didn't get any presents, they'd only have themselves to blame, and I agreed! Then she asked me what I'd be doing on Christmas Day.

"Well, Miss, when I wake up in the morning, I'll look round and see what presents I've got, and I'll play with them and I'll empty my stocking, and usually there are some sweets so I'll eat them, and when I've played a bit more I'll go and wake my mum up and show her what I've got, and then I'll wake my Auntie Doreen – she always stays with us every Christmas; and then after breakfast I'll play a bit more, and then we'll have Christmas dinner, and then we'll go to my grandad's and

I'll play a bit more there, and then I'll go home to bed, and that'll be the end!"

Miss Taylor said that all sounded very nice and she hoped everybody would have such a nice Christmas, but she was surprised I wasn't going to church. Well, I told her that there wouldn't really be time because my grandad likes us to be there early to hear Wilfred Pickles on the wireless visiting a hospital, and to listen to the Queen talking, and then the bell went for home-time and Miss Taylor said we could all go quietly and told us not to forget our stuff for the party.

I went with Tony to get our coats from the cloakroom. Everybody was talking about the party and Barry was there shouting out that their class was going to have the best table because their teacher had made them a Christmas pudding with money in it! I told him that was nothing because Miss Taylor had given everybody in our class sixpence, but he didn't believe me.

"Gerraway, you bloomin' fibber."

"She did, didn't she, Tony?"

Tony shook his head.

"Did she heckers like – she wouldn't give 'owt away."

Huh! You'd think Tony'd've helped me kid Barry along.

"Well, she bought all our Christmas decorations for the classroom . . ." and I went to get my coat. I took my gloves out of my pocket and they were still soaking wet from snowballing at playtime, so I thought I'd put them on the pipes to dry.

"Hey, Tony, my gloves are still sodden."

"Well put 'em on the pipes."

"Yeh, that's a good idea."

While they dried I sat on the pipes. Ooh, it was lovely and warm. There's a window above the basins and I could see the snow was still coming down, really thickly now.

"Hey, it isn't half going to be deep tomorrow."

Everybody had gone now except for Barry, Tony and me. Tony was standing on the basins looking out of the window and Barry

was doing up his coat. It has a hood on it. I wish I had one like it. I could see through the door into the main hall where the Christmas tree was. It looked lovely. Ever so big. It was nearly up to the ceiling.

"Hey, isn't it a big Christmas tree?" Tony jumped down from the basin and came over to where I was sitting.

"Yeh. It's smashing. All them coloured balls. Isn't it lovely, eh, Barry?"

Barry came over.

"Not bad. C'mon you two, let's get going,

eh? C'mon."

"Just a sec, let's see if my gloves are dry."

They weren't really but I put them on. As I was fastening my coat, Barry said how about going carol singing to get a bit of money.

Tony was quite keen, but I didn't know. I mean, my mum'd be expecting me home round about now.

"I suppose *you* can't come because your mum'll be cross with you, as usual!"

Huh. It's all right for Barry. His mum and dad aren't bothered where he goes.

"Course I'll come. Where do you want to go?"

Barry said down near the woods where the posh live, but Tony said it was useless there because they never gave you nowt. So we decided to go round Belgrave Road way, where it's only *quite* posh. It takes about ten minutes to get to Belgrave Road from our school and on the way we argued about which carols to sing. I wanted *Away in a Manger* but Barry wanted *O Come all Ye Faithful*.

"*Away in a Manger* isn't half as good as *O Come all Ye Faithful*, is it, Tony?"

Tony shrugged his shoulders.

"I quite like *Once in Royal David's City.*"

In the end we decided to take it in turns to choose. Belgrave Road's ever so long and we started at number three with *O Come all Ye Faithful.*

"O come all ye faithful, joyful and trium—"

That was as far as we got. A bloke opened the door, gave us three halfpence and told us to push off.

Tony was disgusted.

"That's a good start, halfpenny each."

Barry told him to stop grumbling.

"It's better than nothing. C'mon."

We went on to number five and Tony and Barry started quarrelling again because Tony said it was his turn to choose, but Barry wanted his go again because we'd only sung one line. So we did *O Come all Ye Faithful* again.

"O come all ye faithful, joyful and triumphant, O—"

We didn't get any further this time either. An old lady opened the door and said her mother was poorly so could we sing a bit quieter. We started once more but she stopped us again and said it was still just a little bit too loud and could we sing it quieter.

"O come all ye faithful, joyful and triumphant,

O come ye, o come ye to Bethlehem . . ."

And we sang the whole thing like that, in whispers. We could hardly hear each other. I felt daft and started giggling and that set Tony and Barry off, but the old lady didn't seem to notice. She just stood there while we sang and when we finished she said thank you and gave us twopence each.

At the next house we sang *Once in Royal David's City* right through and then rang the doorbell, but nobody came. We missed number nine out because it was empty and up for sale, and at number eleven we sang *Away in a Manager*.

We went to the end of the road singing every carol we knew. We must've made about a pound between us by the time we got to the other end, and Barry said how about going back and doing the other side of the road. I was all for it, but I just happened to see St Chad's clock. Bloomin' heck! Twenty to nine! I couldn't believe it. I thought it'd be about half-past six, if that. Twenty to nine!

"Hey, I'd better get going. It's twenty to nine. My mum'll kill me!"

The other two said they were going to do a bit more carol singing, so they gave me my share of the money and I ran home as fast as I could. I took a short cut through the snicket behind the fish and chip shop and I got home in about five minutes. I could see my mum standing outside the front door talking to Mrs Theabould, our next-door neighbour. She saw me and walked towards me. I tried to act all calm as if it was only about half-past five or six o'clock.

"Hello, Mum, I've been carol singing."

She gave me a clout. She nearly knocked me over. Right on my freezing cold ear an' all.

"Get inside, you! I've been going mad with worry. Do you know what time it is? Nine o'clock. Get inside!"

She pushed me inside and I heard her thank Mrs Theabould and come in after me. I thought she was going to give me another clout, but she just shouted at me, saying that I was lucky she didn't get the police out, and why didn't I tell her where I was? By this time I was crying my head off.

"But I was only bloomin' carol singing."

"I'll give you carol singing. Get off to bed," and she pushed me upstairs into my bedroom.

"But what about my jelly for tomorrow? Have you made it?"

I thought she was going to go mad.

"Jelly! I'll give you jelly. If you think I've nothing better to do than make jellies while you're out roaming the streets! Get to bed!"

"But I've told Miss Taylor I'm bringing a jelly. I've got to have one. Please, Mum."

She just told me to wash my hands and face and get to bed.

"And if I hear another word out of you, you'll get such a good hiding, you'll wish you hadn't come home," and she went downstairs.

I didn't dare say another word. What was I

going to do about my jelly? I had to bring one. I'd promised. There was only one thing for it. I'd have to make one myself. So I decided to wait until my mum went to bed, and then I'd go downstairs and make one. I don't know how I kept awake. I'm sure I nodded off once or twice, but after a while I heard my mum switch her light out, and when I'd given her enough time to get to sleep, I crept downstairs.

I've seen my mum make jellies tons of times and I knew you had to have boiling water, so I put the kettle on. I looked in the cupboard for a jelly and at first I thought I'd had it, but I found one and emptied it into a glass bowl. It was a funny jelly. Not like the ones my mum usually has. It was sort of like a powder. Still, it said jelly on the packet, so it was all right. A new flavour most likely. I poured the hot water into the bowl, closed the cupboard door, switched off the light, and took the jelly upstairs and I put it under my bed. I could hear my mum snoring so I knew I was all right, and I went to sleep.

Next thing I heard was my mum shouting from downstairs.

"C'mon, get up or you'll be late for school."

I got up and pulled the jelly from under the bed. It had set lovely. All wobbly. But it was a bit of a funny colour, sort of yellowy-white. Still, I'd got my jelly and that's what mattered. My mum didn't say much when I got downstairs. She just told me to eat my breakfast and get to school, so I did. When I'd finished I put my coat on and said ta-ra to my mum in the kitchen and went off. But first I sneaked upstairs and got my jelly and wrapped it in a piece of newspaper.

The first thing we had to do at school was to take what we'd brought for the party into the main hall and stick on a label with our name on it and leave it on the table. Norbert Lightowler was there with his polony sandwiches and mixed pickles. So was Neville Bastowe. Neville Bastowe said that my jelly was a bit funny-looking, but Norbert said he loved jelly more than anything else and he could eat all the jellies in the world.

73

Miss Taylor came along then and told us to take our coats off and go to our classroom. The party wasn't starting till twelve o'clock, so in the morning we played games and sang carols and Miss Taylor read us a story.

Then we had a long playtime and we had a snowball fight with 2B, and I went on the slides until old Wilkie, that's the caretaker, came and put ashes on the ice. Then the bell went and we all had to go to our tables in the main hall. At every place was a Christmas cracker, and everybody had a streamer, but Mr Dyson, the Headmaster, said that we couldn't throw any streamers until we'd finished eating. I pulled my cracker with Tony and got a red paper hat and a pencil sharpener. Tony got a blue hat and a small magnifying glass. When everybody had pulled their crackers we said grace and started eating. I started with a sausage roll that Neville Bastowe had brought, and a polony sandwich.

Miss Taylor had shared my jelly out in bowls and Jennifer Greenwood said it looked horrible and she wasn't going to have any. So did Freda Holdsworth. But Norbert was already on his jelly and said it was lovely and he'd eat anybody else's. Tony started his jelly and spat it out.

"Ugh, it's horrible."

I tasted mine, and it *was* horrible, but I forced it down.

"It's not that bad."

Just then Tony said he could see my mum.

"Isn't that your mum over there?"

He pointed to the door. She was talking to Miss Taylor and they both came over.

"Your mother says you forgot your jelly this morning, here it is."

Miss Taylor put a lovely red jelly on the table. It had bananas and cream on it, and bits of orange. My mum asked me where I'd got my jelly from. I told her I'd made it. I thought she'd be cross, but she and Miss Taylor just laughed and told us to enjoy ourselves, and then my mum went off. Everybody put their hands up for a portion of my mum's jelly – except Norbert.

"I don't want any of that. This is lovely. What flavour is it?"

I told him it was a new flavour and I'd never heard of it before.

"Well, what's it called?"

"Aspic."

"Y'what?"

"Aspic jelly – it's a new flavour!"

Norbert ate the whole thing and was sick afterwards, and everybody else had some of my mum's. It was a right good party.

On the Banks of Plum Creek

Laura Ingalls-Wilder

Monday morning came. As soon as Laura and Mary had washed the breakfast dishes, they went up the ladder and put on their Sunday dresses. Mary's was a blue-sprigged calico, and Laura's was red-sprigged.

Ma braided their hair very tightly and bound the ends with thread. They could not wear their Sunday hair-ribbons because they might lose them. They put on their sun-bonnets, freshly washed and ironed.

Then Ma took them into the bedroom. She knelt down by the box where she kept her best things, and she took out three books. They were the books she had studied when she was a little girl. One was a speller, and one was a reader, and one was a 'rithmetic.

She looked solemnly at Mary and Laura, and they were solemn too.

"I am giving you these books for your very own, Mary and Laura," Ma said. "I know you will take care of them and study them faithfully."

"Yes, Ma," they said.

She gave Mary the books to carry. She gave Laura the little tin pail with their lunch in it, under a clean cloth.

"Goodbye," she said. "Be good girls."

Ma and Carrie stood in the doorway, and Jack went with them down the knoll. He was puzzled. They went on across the grass where the tracks of Pa's wagon wheels went, and Jack stayed close beside Laura.

When they came to the ford of the creek, he sat down and whined anxiously. Laura had to explain to him that he must not come any farther. She stroked his big head and tried to smooth out the worried wrinkles. But he sat watching and frowning while they waded across the shallow, wide ford.

They waded carefully and did not splash their clean dresses. A blue heron rose from the water, flapping away with his long legs dangling. Laura and Mary stepped carefully on to the grass. They would not walk in the dusty wheel tracks until their feet were dry, because their feet must be clean when they came to town.

The new house looked small on its knoll

with the great green prairie spreading far around it. Ma and Carrie had gone inside. Only Jack sat watching by the ford.

Mary and Laura walked on quietly.

Dew was sparkling on the grass. Meadow larks were singing. Snipes were walking on their long, thin legs. Prairie hens were clucking and tiny prairie chicks were peeping. Rabbits stood up with paws dangling, long ears twitching, and their round eyes staring at Mary and Laura.

Pa had said that town was only two and a half miles away, and the road would take them to it. They would know they were in town when they came to a house.

Large white clouds sailed in the enormous sky and their grey shadows trailed across the waving prairie grasses. The road always ended a little way ahead, but when they came to that ending, the road was going on. It was only the tracks of Pa's wagon through the grass.

"For pity's sake, Laura," said Mary, "keep your sunbonnet on! You'll be brown as an

Indian, and what will the town girls think of us?"

"I don't care!" said Laura, loudly and bravely.

"You do too!" said Mary.

"I don't either!" said Laura.

"You do!"

"I don't!"

"You're just as scared of town as I am," said Mary.

Laura did not answer. After a while she took hold of her sunbonnet strings and pulled the bonnet up over her head.

"Anyway, there's two of us," Mary said.

They went on and on. After a long time they saw town. It looked like small blocks of wood on the prairie. When the road dipped down, they saw only grasses again and the sky. Then they saw the town again, always larger. Smoke went up from its stovepipes.

The clean, grassy road ended in dust. This dusty road went by a small house and then past a store. The store had a porch with steps going up to it.

Beyond the store there was a blacksmith's shop. It stood back from the road, with a bare place in front of it. Inside it a big man in a leather apron made a bellows puff! puff! at red coals. He took a white-hot iron out of the coals with tongs, and swung a big hammer down on it, whang! Dozens of sparks flew out, tiny in the daylight.

Beyond the bare place was the back of a building. Mary and Laura walked close to the side of this building. The ground was hard there. There was no more grass to walk on.

In front of this building, another wide, dusty road crossed their road. Mary and Laura stopped. They looked across the dust at the fronts of two more stores. They heard a confused noise of children's voices. Pa's road did not go any farther.

"Come on," said Mary, low. But she stood still. "It's the school where we hear the hollering. Pa said we would hear it."

Laura wanted to turn around and run all the way home.

She and Mary went slowly walking out into

the dust and turned towards that noise of voices. They went padding along between two stores. They passed piles of boards and shingles; that must be the lumber-yard where Pa got the boards for the new house. Then they saw the schoolhouse.

It was out on the prairie beyond the end of the dusty road. A long path went towards it through the grass. Boys and girls were in front of it.

Laura went along the path towards them and Mary came behind her. All those girls and boys stopped their noise and looked. Laura kept on going nearer and nearer all those eyes, and suddenly, without meaning to, she swung the dinner-pail and called out, "You all sounded just like a flock of prairie chickens!"

They were surprised. But they were not as much surprised as Laura. She was ashamed too. Mary gasped, "Laura!" Then a freckled boy with fire-coloured hair yelled, "Snipes, yourselves! Snipes! Snipes! Long-legged snipes!"

Laura wanted to sink down and hide her legs. Her dress was too short, it was much shorter than the town girls' dresses. So was Mary's. Before they came to Plum Creek, Ma had said they were outgrowing those dresses. Their bare legs did look long and spindly, like snipes' legs.

All the boys were pointing and yelling, "Snipes! Snipes!"

Then a red-headed girl began pushing those boys and saying: "Shut up! You make too much noise! Shut up, Sandy!" she said to the red-headed boy, and he shut up. She came close to Laura and said:

"My name is Christy Kennedy, and that horrid boy is my brother Sandy, but he doesn't mean any harm. What's your name?"

Her red hair was braided so tightly that the braids were stiff. Her eyes were dark blue, almost black, and her round cheeks were freckled. Her sunbonnet hung down her back.

"Is that your sister?" she said. "Those are my sisters." Some big girls were talking to Mary. "The big one's Nettie, and the black-haired one's Cassie, and then there's Donald and me and Sandy. How many brothers and sisters have you?"

"Two," Laura said. "That's Mary, and Carrie's the baby. She has golden hair too. And we have a bulldog named Jack. We live on Plum Creek. Where do you live?"

"Does your Pa drive two bay horses with black manes and tails?" Christy asked.

"Yes," said Laura. "They are Sam and David, our Christmas horses."

"He comes by our house, so you came by it too," said Christy. "It's the house before you came to Beadle's store and post-office, before you get to the blacksmith shop. Miss Eva Beadle's our teacher. That's Nellie Oleson."

Nellie Oleson was very pretty. Her yellow hair hung in long curls, with two big blue ribbon bows on top. Her dress was thin white lawn, with little blue flowers scattered over it, and she wore shoes.

She looked at Laura and she looked at Mary, and she wrinkled up her nose.

"Hmm!" she said. "Country girls!"

Before anyone else could say anything, a bell rang. A young lady stood in the schoolhouse doorway, swinging the bell in her hand. All the boys and girls hurried by her into the schoolhouse.

She was a beautiful young lady. Her brown hair was frizzed in bangs over her brown eyes, and done in thick braids behind. Buttons sparkled all down the front of her bodice, and her skirts were drawn back tightly and fell down behind in big puffs and loops. Her face was sweet and her smile was lovely.

She laid her hand on Laura's shoulder and said, "You're a new little girl, aren't you?"

"Yes, ma'am," said Laura.

"And is this your sister?" Teacher asked, smiling at Mary.

"Yes, ma'am," said Mary.

"Then come with me," said Teacher, "and I'll write your names in my book."

They went with her the whole length of the schoolhouse, and stepped up on the platform.

The schoolhouse was a room made of new boards. Its ceiling was the underneath of shingles, like the attic ceiling. Long benches stood one behind another down the middle of the room. They were made of planed boards. Each bench had a back, and two shelves stuck out from the back, over the bench behind. Only the front bench did not have any shelves in front of it, and the last bench did not have any back.

There were two glass windows in each side of the schoolhouse. They were open, and so was the door. The wind came in, and the sound of waving grasses, and the smell and the sight of the endless prairie and the great light of the sky.

Laura saw all this while she stood with Mary by Teacher's desk and they told her their names and how old they were. She did not move her head, but her eyes looked around.

A water-pail stood on a bench by the door. A bought broom stood in one corner. On the wall behind Teacher's desk there was a smooth space of boards painted black. Under it was a little trough. Some kind of short,

white sticks lay in the trough, and a block of wood with a woolly bit of sheepskin pulled tightly around it and nailed down. Laura wondered what those things were.

Mary showed Teacher how much she could read and spell. But Laura looked at Ma's book and shook her head. She could not read. She was not even sure of all the letters.

"Well, you can begin at the beginning, Laura," said Teacher, "and Mary can study further on. Have you a slate?"

They did not have a slate.

"I will lend you mine," Teacher said. "You cannot learn to write without a slate."

She lifted up the top of her desk and took out the slate. The desk was made like a tall box, with one side cut out for her knees. The top rose up on bought hinges, and under it was the place where she kept things. Her books were there, and the ruler.

Laura did not know until later that the ruler was to punish anyone who fidgeted or whispered in school. Anyone who was so naughty had to walk up to Teacher's desk and hold out her hand while Teacher slapped it many times, hard, with the ruler.

But Laura and Mary never whispered in school, and they always tried not to fidget. They sat side by side on a bench and studied. Mary's feet rested on the floor, but Laura's dangled. They held their book open on the board shelf before them, Laura studying at the front of the book and Mary studying farther on, and the pages between standing straight up.

Laura was a whole class by herself, because

she was the only pupil who could not read. Whenever Teacher had time, she called Laura to her desk and helped her read letters. Just before dinner-time that first day, Laura was able to read, C A T, cat. Suddenly she remembered and said, "P A T, Pat!"

Teacher was surprised.

"R A T, rat!" said Teacher. "M A T, mat!" And Laura was reading! She could read the whole first row in the speller.

At noon all the other children and Teacher went home to dinner. Laura and Mary took their dinner-pail and sat in the grass against the shady side of the empty schoolhouse. They ate their bread and butter and talked.

"I like school," Mary said.

"So do I," said Laura. "Only it makes my legs tired. But I don't like that Nellie Oleson that called us country girls."

"We are country girls," said Mary.

"Yes, and she needn't wrinkle her nose!" Laura said.

What's Watt?

Steve Barlow and Steve Skidmore

"**S**cience!" groaned John Watt. "I hate science."

John was standing outside a grim-looking brown door. Through the layers of age-old paint, the words *Science Laboratory 1* were just about visible to the naked eye. The writing was done in faded gold and old-fashioned letters. Frankenstein's laboratory probably had a sign just like it. John squinted at his new timetable to check he was in the right place at the right time. He hoped he'd got it wrong. He hadn't.

– ELMLEY SCHOOL –
Monday, Period One: Science –
Mr Allen in Science Lab 1

Science! It wasn't much of an incentive to wake up on a Monday morning, thought John. He couldn't quite picture himself leaping out of bed at the crack of dawn yelling, "Oh yippee, thank goodness the weekend's over, I must rush to school to get to my science lesson!" Although, thinking about it, John couldn't picture himself leaping out of bed at the crack of dawn on any morning. Going to school wasn't an incentive to get out of bed, full stop. Especially going to a new school where he didn't know anyone.

John stood for a moment, thinking about what future diseases and illnesses he could try to convince his mother he had caught in order to avoid:

a) Science on a Monday morning and

b) School, on every other morning . . .

Mumps, flu, veruccas and bubonic plague sprang to mind, but he knew his mum would just say something like, "Really, dear, you've caught bubonic plague? Oh, how terrible for you. Well, off you go to school and I hope you don't die."

Eventually, John summoned up his courage, knocked on the door and entered the lab.

"Yes?"

John assumed the strange-looking figure standing at the front of the lab, pointing at some meaningless squiggles on a whiteboard, was Mr Allen, Teacher of Science, Elmley School, Monday, period one.

"I'm new," squeaked John. "It's my first day."

Mr Allen peered over his half-rim glasses.

"A new student in the summer term? Hmm, I wasn't told about this. But of course, they never tell me anything, I'm always the last to know. Not like the old days, not when I was doing the timetable . . ."

John stood still, wondering what he should do as Mr Allen continued grumbling to himself. John was aware that the class was staring at him. He began to fidget.

Mr Allen stopped muttering and fixed John with a stare. "Well, it's not your fault, I suppose. Your name?"

"Watt," said John.

"Your name?" repeated Mr Allen.

"Watt," repeated John.

"Are you deaf?" Mr Allen grunted. "What's your name?"

"That's right."

"What's right?" Mr Allen looked bemused.

"Yes, it is," said John, smiling encouragingly.

"What is?"

"Watt is," explained John helpfully, or so he

thought. Some of the class began to giggle.

Mr Allen stared hard at John. A flush of red began to travel up his neck and into his cheeks. "Your first day and you're being rude to a teacher?"

John was confused. Being rude? He wasn't being rude. "I'm not," he replied.

"Not what?" Mr Allen was beginning to twitch.

John took a deep breath. "No, I *am* Watt."

Mr Allen's red flush was rapidly shooting up his forehead. He's going to explode, thought John, I'd better try and stop this. But how? Luckily, his mouth took over from his brain and came up with the answer. "My name is John Watt, sir," John heard himself call out.

"Oh." Mr Allen paused. The red flush began to retreat. "Why didn't you say so?"

John stared at him. "I did, sir. Lots of times."

The flush started upwards again. "Are you contradicting me?"

"No, sir!"

"I've got my eye on you, Watt. Sit down."
Mr Allen, breathing heavily, turned back to
the board.

John glanced nervously at the rest of the
class. From the dense undergrowth of gas
taps, DC power connectors, curved laboratory
taps, test tubes and beakers, a forest of faces
loomed. Not one of them was familiar, and
they were all staring at him. Judging and
forming an opinion of him. Probably not a
good one, thought John.

"Over there, get a move on!" Mr Allen's
barked order brought John back to his
senses. Mr Allen was pointing towards the
back of the class where there was a boy
sitting at a bench on his own.

John scuttled over. The forest of faces
followed John on his brief journey, then
obeyed Mr Allen's command to "Look this
way!" and turned back towards the
whiteboard.

The boy sitting on his own looked up at
John as if he wasn't sure it was worth the
effort. He nodded towards the empty stool

next to him to indicate where John should sit.

"I'm Bright," he said.

What a bighead, thought John as he scrutinized his new neighbour. He looked fairly normal. Except for his hair. John had never seen anything like it. It stood out at every conceivable angle, and at a few that defied the known laws of geometry. It looked as though he'd been in a fight with a mad gorilla armed with several tubes of exploding hair gel.

John suddenly realized he was staring, so he nodded a half-hearted hello and sat down.

As he reached into his bag for his pencil case, he gave out a sigh. What a start! And all because of his name. Just like it had been at his old school. "Watt's what?", "Watt a laugh", "Watt are you doing?", "Watt's the answer?" If he'd heard the pun once, he'd heard it a million times.

In his innocence, John had thought that a new start would mean no more name trouble. That thought had been the only good thing about moving.

"We're going away," his mum had said. "A new town; a new job for me; a new school for you. A new start for us."

John had wanted to tell his mum that he didn't want the new. The new scared him and, despite the teasing about his name, he was quite happy with the old, thank you very much. But when his dad had left home "because things weren't working out" and his mum had decided that she and John needed a "new start", John didn't have the heart to argue.

As his thoughts continued to drift, John was suddenly shocked back to the present as he heard Mr Allen's voice calling his name.

He sat bolt upright. "Yes, sir?"

"What?" Mr Allen scowled.

"Yes, sir? Did you want me?" asked John, in all innocence.

"I wasn't talking to you!" snapped Mr Allen.

"But you said 'Watt'," John said.

Mr Allen's flush returned with a vengeance. "I wasn't talking to you and I didn't say 'Watt', I said 'what' to someone else who was asking a question, because I didn't hear what he was saying, Watt!" cried the exasperated teacher.

John's mind was reeling. "What?"

"Don't start that again!" Mr Allen's flush had turned a nasty purple colour.

"Sorry," mumbled John. He swore he could hear the sniggers of his new classmates.

Mr Allen rounded on John. "Well, you obviously weren't paying attention. Can you tell me the subject matter with which we are dealing?"

John looked blank. He was in big trouble and he knew it.

"Units of electricity," hissed the boy next to him.

"Units of electricity!" repeated John, glad of the lifeline that had been thrown him.

Mr Allen looked disappointed that John had been able to answer. "Er, yes, correct. Units of electricity: the amp, the volt, the ohm and the watt . . ." He pointed a quivering finger at John. "*And don't you dare say a word or you will live to regret it*!"

John sat and gawped at him.

"So," said Mr Allen, through gritted teeth, "let's see how much our new pupil knows." The whole class turned to stare at John. He gulped.

Mr Allen growled, "What's a watt, Watt?"

The class burst into gales of laughter. Mr Allen, realizing too late what he had just said, turned beetroot-coloured. As the classroom rocked with laughter, John felt a horrible urge to giggle creep over him. The feeling was quickly squashed and replaced by a huge stomach-churning spasm as Mr Allen turned his fury on the hapless newcomer.

"Watt!" roared Mr Allen. "You're in detention!"

The Boy Who Could Tell the Future

Rob Marsh

It all began during P.T. one day. We were in the gym and Mr Jacobs, the P.T. teacher, had dragged out the vaulting-horse to show us how to do a hand-spring. There was a glint in his eye which made us all very nervous because we knew from experience that when he was enthusiastic about something, it spelt danger. We didn't realize how true that would be until a few moments later.

After he had gathered us all around him, Mr Jacobs then continued to tell us how to perform the exercise.

"It's a very simple vault," he explained.

"You run and jump on the wooden spring-board which I have carefully positioned for that purpose. Then stretch forwards with your arms and push yourself off the top of the vaulting-horse.

"Throw your legs over your head and land feet first on the big rubber mat beyond. What could be easier than that?"

We all swallowed in terror.

"Your job," he continued, "is simple. And my job is to stand in the landing area and ensure that no one is killed in the process."

He flashed his teeth at us then, so we could see that this was just his little joke.

"You're going to enjoy this," he said.

We exchanged glances and moved our weight uncomfortably from one foot to the other.

"Line up!" he ordered.

For a few seconds we milled around in confusion as everyone tried to get to the back of the queue. Eventually, he intervened. "Sissies!" he shouted. "You're all a bunch of sissies! Let me show you how it's done."

He strode forward to where we were standing, shame-faced with embarrassment.

He pushed some of us aside and turned to begin his run. He hit the spring-board hard enough to make some of us flinch, did a perfect flip-over, and landed feet together and upright. It was a good vault and earned him a round of spontaneous applause.

We were impressed. There was no doubt about it. We were still not that eager to attempt that feat ourselves, but we were impressed all the same. If a teacher could do it, surely we could!

"Now who is going to be first?" he asked.

Patrick Lee put his hand up. "I'd like to have a go, sir," he said. Patrick was eleven at the time, like the rest of us. He was tall and gawky like me and had long, straight black hair that kept falling forward over his eyes. I only met his parents once. They were really nice people. His dad was from Durban and ran a computer business and his mother was from Paarl in the Cape and taught Afrikaans. It wasn't until that moment that I suspected there was insanity in the family!

"Step forward," Mr Jacobs said and took up his position near the landing-zone. Like a bull about to charge, Patrick lowered his head, rocked backwards on his heels once, twice, three times and then set off like a bullet.

We could all see that he was going to overshoot even before he hit the spring-board. He never got his head up properly for one thing, and he was going too fast for another. He just took off and seemed to keep going. He never even touched the vaulting-horse. He just went right over the top, arms and legs flailing in the air, straight at Mr Jacobs who, of course, was expecting him.

Suddenly, there was a look of horror on the teacher's face. He braced himself to do his duty and caught one of Patrick's swinging fists between the eyes.

"Ooh!" he groaned loudly. Then he was hit by the rest of the flying body. They collapsed on the ground together where they writhed for a few seconds like an octopus having a fit.

By the time we'd all rushed over, all the twitching had stopped and they were lying as still as corpses on the floor. Eventually they began moving again, moaning as they did so and rose groggily to their feet. There was a trickle of blood running from Mr Jacobs's large nose and his eyes were hideously bloodshot. Patrick was clutching a lump on the back of his neck which was the size of a bird's egg.

Helped by the rest of us, they limped off to the changing-rooms.

That, of course, was the end of the lesson and we never did learn how to do a handspring. But it's not the end of the story. In fact, it was actually the beginning, though I didn't realize it until two weeks later.

At ten o'clock on the morning before exams were due to start, Mr Bailey, the Headmaster, interrupted lessons to call an emergency school assembly. When the hall was full and we were all quietly seated, he strode in looking very grave and took his place on the stage in front of the other teachers.

"Boys and girls," he began, glaring down at us over the top of his spectacles, "I have some very bad news for you . . ." There was a long pause and everyone held their breath. "We are going to have to cancel this term's exams."

A big cheer would have gone up then, but his look forewarned us. Instead, there was a ripple of excited movement as children shifted in their seats waiting for an explosion from the Headmaster.

"The key to the school strong-room in

which all the exam papers are being held for safe-keeping, has been mislaid. Both myself and the staff have searched everywhere, but without success. We now have to call in an expert locksmith.

"Unfortunately, the man in question is out of town for the next week. Under the circumstances it is simply not possible to complete the exam programme before the end of term. For this reason, we have decided to defer all examinations until next term . . ."

When the Headmaster had first started speaking, Patrick had suddenly stood up and put his arm in the air. At first Mr Bailey had paid him no attention and some of the teachers standing down the sides of the hall had hissed at him to sit down. Instead, he remained as he was, arms upraised, determined and motionless like a statue.

Eventually, when the Headmaster decided he could ignore the interruption no longer, he turned his angry gaze on Patrick.

"Can't you see I'm speaking, Lee?" he asked.

Patrick put his hand down. "Yes, sir, but I think I know where the key is, sir."

A murmur of interest ran around the hall, which was silenced swiftly by the Headmaster's bellowed "Silence!"

A deathly hush fell over the proceedings once more. He shifted from one foot to another.

"What do you mean, Lee? Explain yourself clearly, my boy . . ."

"As I said, sir. I think I know where the key is."

"How do you know?"

For the first time since he had stood up Patrick looked a bit uncomfortable. He shrugged. "I just know, sir, that's all. Have you looked down the side of the chair in your office? I think it slipped out of your pocket two days ago, sir."

Everyone burst out laughing then and even Mr Bailey showed his teeth, but it was hardly a smile.

"Sit down, you foolish boy!" he said and, leading the teachers out behind him, marched off into the long and gloomy corridor.

Apart from the teasing Patrick got from the rest of us, that would have been the end of the matter except that twenty minutes later the door to our classroom was thrown open violently by an excited Mr Bailey. He had the missing key held up before him.

"How did you know where it was, Lee?" he demanded without so much as a "Good morning, class". "Did you put it there?"

Patrick stood firm. He shook his head with such obvious innocence even the Headmaster could see he wasn't lying. "No, sir. Somehow I just knew where it was, that's all, sir . . ."

For a few seconds, Mr Bailey eyed him suspiciously, opened his mouth as if to say something, then shut it once more. "Exams begin tomorrow as planned," he announced. Then he spun on his heel and departed.

Above the collective groan from the class, the voice of one pupil rang out clearly. It was Big Mike. "I'm going to get you for that, Lee," he hissed threateningly, "I'm really going to get you. You have spoilt everything!"

Now, Big Mike was not the sort of boy you would want to cross. Being fourteen in a class full of eleven-year-olds made him think that he could inflict pain freely on to others as his special privilege. It was his way of exercising control.

I was witness to his vengeance two days later. When I walked into the gym changing-rooms just after break-time, Patrick was sitting on the floor, a dribble of blood oozing from a fat lip. Big Mike was leaning over him, fists clenched for action and the rest of the class was standing to one side, silent as trees in a forest.

"Get up, Lee," Big Mike said, shoving him hard with his foot.

It was as if Patrick didn't seem to notice him. He touched a finger to his mouth and winced slightly at the pain.

"Get up!" Big Mike repeated, a more threatening tone creeping into his voice. In fact, he would've booted him again where he sat if I hadn't stepped in then.

"Lay off him, Mike," I said.

Trying to tell Big Mike what to do was like showing a red rag to a bull. But I was the one who used to help him with his homework, so I hoped this meant I had a special kind of licence to say things to him nobody else would dare to.

Big Mike announced he was going to thump Patrick again so we argued the pros and cons of beating him to a pulp for a couple of minutes then I reasoned with him and he finally backed down, muttering death threats as he walked away. I helped Patrick get to his feet while everyone else drifted off to get changed.

"Thanks," he said.

"I'm sorry that happened," I said, "but don't report him. It'll only make things worse if you do."

He smiled sadly, or at least tried to, given the fact that his mouth wasn't working properly.

"I won't add to his problems," he mumbled. "Big Mike'll have more than enough to worry

111

about before long."

It seemed a funny thing to say. I wasn't sure if it wasn't some kind of threat. If it was a threat then I assumed it was just big talk to save face so I didn't think much about it at the time. I only remembered what he'd said a couple of days later when I heard that Big Mike's parents had been injured in a car crash.

They eventually recovered, but for the next six months Big Mike seemed to spend most of his time going backwards and forwards to the hospital to see them and he never did give anyone a hard time after that.

It wasn't long after the "Big Mike" incident that Patrick started acting strangely. He used to go and sit on his own in the playground during break-times. He would either read a book or just stare off into space. A couple of times I even went over to him and tried to keep him company. I could see that although he was very polite, he didn't really care if anyone talked to him or not, so in the end I didn't bother any more.

One day, when we were walking home together, Patrick suddenly said, "I hit my head when I tried that vault, you know."

"I know you did," I said.

He went silent for a moment after that and I could see from the look on his face that he was deciding whether or not to tell me something.

"Yes, but, the thing is, I think it did something to me. I mean, I can see things, well . . . more clearly now."

I had no idea what he was talking about. "You can see things . . . clearly?" I said.

"Yes. Future things."

"Future things?"

"Yes. Sometimes I know what is going to happen before it does."

"But that's impossible!"

He nodded in agreement. "I know it's impossible but I can do it. That's how I knew about the key and Big Mike's parents."

I didn't quite know what to say after that. I don't think he did either, so we both fell silent again. I remember, though, that it crossed my

113

mind that maybe the blow on the head had affected his mind, but not in the way he claimed. I was much too good a friend to tell him this.

"Tell me what's coming up in tomorrow's History exam, then," I said, thinking that would throw him. It didn't. He just reached into his bag and pulled out a sheet of notepaper on which he had written a long list of questions. "Maybe you should study these," he said and smiled weakly.

Well, the question came up. Every last one of them. Word for word! It was almost as if he'd copied them off the exam paper himself.

After school, I couldn't wait to speak to him. "Tell me how you knew?" I asked.

He shrugged, showing me he didn't want to talk about it. "I told you," he said. "I just see things, that's all."

This didn't seem to be a very good answer to me. First, the Headmaster's safe key, then Big Mike and now the History exam. I just thought he'd found a way to get to the question papers.

"What do you mean, you just see things?" I persisted. I wasn't going to give up on this.

"I see pictures. Sometimes they look like a photograph. Sometimes it looks like two or three seconds from a movie, but with no soundtrack and I just know what is going to happen. I can't explain."

"So, do you see people you know as well?"

He nodded. "I saw the Headmaster, I saw Big Mike . . . I saw . . ." but then he didn't finish. There was a scared look on his face. At that moment I got an uncomfortable feeling deep in the pit of my stomach. Suddenly, I started feeling a bit sick.

"Who else have you seen?" I asked suspiciously.

He didn't answer.

"Have you seen me?" I inquired.

I could tell he didn't want to look me in the face. He continued to stare in front of me.

"Patrick, have you ever seen me?"

"Once," he whispered finally.

I swallowed hard because my mouth had suddenly gone dry. "Once," I repeated.

"When? A year or a month ago? Last night . . .?"

"Last night," he said.

"Last night?"

He nodded.

"What was I doing?"

It took him a long time to answer. "You weren't doing anything. I could only see your face."

"You could only see my face. Was I laughing?"

He shook his head.

"Was I crying?"

"No." There was a long pause this time. "You just looked very scared."

"I just looked very scared?"

He lifted his head and stared at me then. "Yes," he said. "Very scared. There was a name as well."

"A name?"

"Tims. The name was Tims. Who do you know named Tims?"

I didn't know anybody named Tims, but that didn't make me feel any better. All I could think of was Big Mike and the trouble he'd had after Patrick had "seen" him.

"Are you sure it was me?" I said.

But that was one thing he was certain of. "Oh, yes," he replied. "I'm certain."

After school I was still worried and I waited for Patrick outside the school gates so we could catch the school bus together. We were still talking about his "dream" when we got off the main road. I suppose both of us must have been quite distracted. The truth is, I still can't remember all the details about that part of the incident. What I do know is that we stood on the pavement until the bus pulled away and then started to cross.

On the other side of the street, a big furniture truck belonging to a firm named SMIT & SON, was parked outside a shop and the driver was unloading boxes on to the pavement. There was something about the name that caught my attention. That's one of the reasons why I didn't look properly before I stepped off the pavement. Why Patrick wasn't concentrating, I've no idea.

We'd almost reached the other side when a Ford bakkie seemed to come out of nowhere. It didn't actually hit either of us, but its wing mirror brushed Patrick's jacket with enough force to send him staggering. I also remember hearing a screech of brakes and a car hooting its horn at the same time, but the driver never stopped. I still think it was a miracle he didn't get killed.

So does he for that matter!

I just had time to see the look of surprise on Patrick's face, then he collapsed. He seemed to vanish under the SMIT & SON trailer.

I ran around the truck and by the time I got to the pavement on the other side, Patrick was sitting up in the gutter, covered in dust, rubbing the back of his head again.

"Wow, that was close," he said.

I was so scared at that moment, I couldn't answer. I shall never forget though, what I saw when I glanced up into the shop window above him. There was my face in the glass, pinched and drawn with fright, but there was also the name he'd talked about – TIMS. You see, behind me on the pavement was a tall pile of boxes stacked up in the front of the lorry, hiding all but the Smit part of the SMIT & SON name which was painted on the side. The sun was shining on the lorry, making the letters glow and SMIT was being reflected on to the window, but in reverse, of course. His prediction had come true!

That was when I finally realized Patrick really had been able to see into the future. The funny thing is, he never did get any more of his strange dreams once the second bump on his head went down. So that was the end of the story.

And you know something, I think both of us were really, really relieved . . .

Tales of a Fourth Grade Nothing

Judy Blume

In January our class started a project on The City. Mrs Haver, our teacher, divided us up into committees by where we live. That way we could work at home. My committee was me, Jimmy Fargo, and Sheila. Our topic was Transportation. We decided to make my apartment the meeting place because I'm the only one of the three of us who's got his own bedroom. In a few weeks each committee has to hand in a booklet, a poster and be ready to give an oral report.

The first day we got together after school we bought a yellow posterboard. Jimmy wanted a blue one but Sheila talked him out of it. "Yellow is a much brighter colour," she explained. "Everything will show up on it. Blue is too dull!"

Sheila thinks she's smarter than me and Jimmy put together – just because she's a girl! So right away she told us she would be in charge of our booklet and me and Jimmy could do most of the poster. As long as we check with her first, to make sure she likes our ideas. We agreed, since Sheila promised to do ten pages of written work and we would only do five.

After we bought the yellow posterboard we went to the library. We took out seven books on transportation. We wanted to learn all we could about speed, traffic congestion and pollution. We arranged to meet on Tuesday and Thursday afternoons for the next two weeks.

Our first few committee meetings turned out like this: we got to my place by three-thirty, had a snack, then played with Dribble for another half hour. Sheila gave up on cooties when Fudge lost his front teeth. But it still isn't much fun to have her hanging around. She's always complaining that she got stuck with the worst possible committee. And that me and Jimmy fool more than we work. We only put up with her because we have no choice!

Sheila and Jimmy have to be home for supper before five-thirty. So at five o'clock we start cleaning up. We keep our equipment under my bed in a shoe box. We have a set of Magic Markers, Elmer's glue, Scotch tape, a really sharp pair of scissors, and a container of silver sparkle.

Sheila carries our committee booklet back and forth with her. She doesn't trust us enough to leave it at my house! The posterboard fits under my bed, along with our supplies. We stack the library books on my desk. The reason I make sure we clean up good is that my mother told me if I left a mess we'd have to find some place else to work.

By our third meeting I told Jimmy and Sheila that I'd figured out the solution to New

York City's traffic problems. "We have to get rid of the traffic," I said. "There shouldn't be any cars or buses or taxis allowed in the city. What we really need is a citywide monorail system."

"That's too expensive," Sheila said. "It sounds good but it's not practical."

"I disagree!" I told Sheila. "It's very practical. Besides getting rid of traffic it'll get rid of air pollution and it'll get people where they're going a lot faster."

"But it's not practical, Peter!" Sheila said again. "It costs too much."

I opened one of my books on transportation and read Sheila a quote. "'A monorail system is the hope of the future.'" I cleared my throat and looked up.

"But we can't write a report just about the monorail," Sheila said. "We'll never be able to fill twenty written pages with that."

"We can write big," Jimmy suggested.

"No!" Sheila said. "I want a good mark on this project. Peter, you can write your five pages about the monorail system and how it works. Jimmy, you can write your five pages about pollution caused by transportation. And I'll write my ten pages on the history of transportation in the city." Sheila folded her arms and smiled.

"Can I write big?" Jimmy asked.

"I don't care how big you write as long as you put your name on your five pages!" Sheila told him.

"That's not fair!" Jimmy said. "This is supposed to be a group project. Why should I have to put my name on my five pages?"

"Then don't write BIG!" Sheila shouted.

"OK. OK . . . I'll write so small Mrs Haver will need a microscope to see the letters."

"Very funny," Sheila said.

"Look," I told both of them, "I think all our written work should be in the same handwriting. That's the only fair way. Otherwise Mrs Haver will know who did what. And it won't be a group project."

"Say, that's a good idea," Jimmy said. "Which one of us has the best handwriting?"

Me and Jimmy looked at Sheila.

"Well, I do have a nice even script," Sheila said. "But if I'm going to copy over your written work you better give it to me by next Tuesday. Otherwise, I won't have enough time to do the job. And you two better get going on your poster." Sheila talked like she was the teacher and we were the kids.

Me and Jimmy designed the whole poster ourselves. We used the pros and cons of each kind of transportation. It was really clever. We divided a chart into land, sea and air and we planned an illustration for each – with the aeroplane done in silver sparkle and the letters done in red and blue Magic Marker. We got halfway through the lettering that day. We also sketched in the ship, the plane and the truck.

When Sheila saw it she asked, "Is that supposed to be a train?"

"No," I told her. "It's a truck."

"It doesn't look like one," she said.

"It will," Jimmy told her, "when it's finished."

"I hope so," Sheila said. "Because right

now it looks like a flying train!"

"That's because the ground's not under it yet," Jimmy said.

"Yeah," I agreed. "See, we've got to make it look like it's on a street. Right now it does kind of look like it's up in space."

"So does the ship," Sheila said.

"We'll put some water lines around it," I told her.

"And some clouds around the plane," Sheila said.

"Listen," Jimmy hollered, "did anybody ever tell you you're too bossy? This poster is ours! You do the booklet. Remember . . . that's the way you wanted it!"

"See . . . there you go again!" Sheila said. "You keep forgetting this is a committee. We're supposed to work together."

"Working together doesn't mean you give the orders and we carry them out," Jimmy said.

My feelings exactly! I thought.

Sheila didn't answer Jimmy. She picked up her things, got her coat and left.

"I hope she never comes back," Jimmy said.

"She'll be back," I told him. "We're her committee."

Jimmy laughed. "Yeah . . . we're all one happy committee!"

I put our poster under the bed, said goodbye to Jimmy, then washed up for supper.

My mother was being pretty nice about our committee meetings. She arranged to have Fudge play at Ralph's apartment on Tuesdays and at Jennie's on Thursdays. Sam has the chicken pox, so he can't play at all.

I was glad that next week would be our last committee meeting after school. I was sick of Sheila and I was getting sick of Transportation. Besides, now that I knew a monorail system was the only way to save our city I was getting upset that the mayor and all the other guys that run things at City Hall weren't doing anything about installing one. If *I* know that's the best method of city transportation how come *they* don't know it?

The next day when I came home from school I went into my bedroom to see Dribble like I always do. Fudge was in there, sitting on my bed.

"Why are you in my room?" I asked him.

He smiled.

"You know you're not supposed to be in here. This is *my* room."

"Want to see?" Fudge said.

"See what?"

"Want to see?"

"What? What are you talking about?" I asked.

He jumped off my bed and crawled underneath it. He came out with our poster. He held it up. "See," he said. "Pretty!"

"What did you do?" I yelled. "What did you do to our poster?" It was covered all over with scribbles in every colour Magic Marker. It was ruined! *It was a mess and it was ruined*. I was ready to kill Fudge. I grabbed my poster and ran into the kitchen to show it to my mother. I could hardly speak. "Look," I said, feeling a lump in my throat. "Just look at what he did to my poster." I felt tears come to my eyes but I didn't care. "How could you let

him?" I asked my mother. "How? Don't you care about me?"

I threw the poster down and ran into my room. I slammed the door, took off my shoe and flung it at the wall. It made a black mark where it hit. Well, so what!

Soon I heard my mother hollering – and then Fudge crying. After a while my mother knocked on my bedroom door and called, "Peter, may I come in?"

I didn't answer.

She opened the door and walked over to my

bed. She sat down next to me. "I'm very sorry," she said.

I still didn't say anything.

"Peter," she began.

I didn't look at her.

She touched my arm. "Peter . . . please listen . . ."

"Don't you see, Mom? I can't even do my homework without him messing it up. It just isn't fair! I wish he was never born. *Never*! I hate him!"

"You don't hate him," my mother said. "You just think you do."

"Don't tell me," I said. "I mean it. I really can't stand that kid!"

"You're angry," my mother told me. "I know that and I don't blame you. Fudge had no right to touch your poster. I spanked him."

"You did?" I asked. Fudge never gets spanked. My parents don't believe in spanking. "You really spanked him?" I asked again.

"Yes," my mother said.

"Hard?" I asked.

"On his backside," she told me.

I thought that over.

"Peter . . ." My mother put her arm around me. "I'll buy you a new posterboard tomorrow. It was really my fault. I should never have let him into your room."

"That's why I need a lock on my door," I said.

"I don't like locks on doors. We're a family. We don't have to lock each other out."

"If I had a lock Fudge wouldn't have found my poster!"

"It won't happen again," my mother promised.

I wanted to believe her, but really I didn't. Unless she tied him up I knew my brother would get into my room again.

The next day, while I was at school, my mother bought a new yellow posterboard. The hard part was explaining to Jimmy that we had to start all over again. He was a good sport about it. He said this time he'd make sure his truck didn't look like a flying train.

And I said, this time I'd make pencil marks first so my letters didn't go uphill.

Our committee met that afternoon. Sheila didn't mention the last time. Neither did we. Me and Jimmy worked on the poster while Sheila copied our written work into the booklet. We'd be ready to give our oral report to the class on Monday. Not like some committees who hadn't even started yet!

By five o'clock we had finished our poster and Sheila was almost done with the cover for our booklet. Jimmy walked over and stood behind her, watching her work.

After a minute he yelled, "What do you think you're doing, Sheila?"

I got up from the floor and joined them at my desk. I took a look at the cover. It was pretty nice. It said:

TRANSPORTATION IN THE CITY

Under that it said:

BY SHEILA TUBMAN, PETER HATCHER, AND JAMES FARGO

And under that in small letters it said:

handwritten by miss sheila tubman

Now I knew why Jimmy was mad. "Oh no!" I said, holding my hand to my head. "How could you!"

Sheila didn't say anything.

"It's not fair," I told her. "We didn't put our names on the poster!"

"But the cover's all done," Sheila said. "Can't you see that? I'll never get the letters so straight again. It looks perfect!"

"Oh no!" Jimmy shouted. "We're not handing the booklet in like that. I'll rip it up before I let you!" He grabbed the booklet and threatened to tear it in half.

Sheila screamed. "You wouldn't! I'll kill you! Give it back to me, Jimmy Fargo!" She was ready to cry.

I knew Jimmy wouldn't tear it up but I didn't say so.

"Peter . . . make him give it back!"

"Will you take off that line about your handwriting?" I asked.

"I can't. It'll ruin the booklet."

"Then I think he should rip it up," I said.

Sheila stamped her foot. "Ooooh! I hate you both!"

"You don't really," I told her. "You just think you do."

"I know I do!" Sheila cried.

"That's because you're angry right now," I said. I couldn't help smiling.

Sheila jumped up and tried to get the booklet but Jimmy held it over his head and he's much taller than Sheila. She had no

134

chance at all.

Finally she sat down and whispered, "I give up. You win. I'll take my name off."

"You promise?" Jimmy asked.

"I promise," Sheila said.

Jimmy set the booklet down on my desk in front of Sheila. "OK," he said. "Start."

"I'm not going to make a whole new cover," Sheila said. "What I'll do is turn this bottom line into a decoration." She picked up a Magic Marker and made little flowers out of the words. Soon, *handwritten by miss sheila tubman*, turned into sixteen small flowers. "There," Sheila said. "It's done."

"It looks pretty good," I told her.

"It would have looked better without those flowers," Jimmy said. "But at least it's fair now."

That night I showed my mother and father our new poster. They thought it was great. Especially our silver-sparkle aeroplane. My mother put the poster on top of the refrigerator so it would be safe until the next day, when I would take it to school.

Now I had nothing to worry about. Sheila had the booklet, the poster was safe and our committee was finished before schedule. I went into my room to relax. Fudge was sitting on the floor, near my bed. My shoebox of supplies was in front of him. His face was a mess of magic marker colours and he was using my extra sharp scissors to snip away at his hair. And the hair he snipped was dropping into Dribble's bowl – which he had in front of him on the floor!

"See," he said. "See Fudge. Fudgie's a barber!"

That night I found out hair doesn't hurt my turtle. I picked off every strand from his shell. I cleaned out his bowl and washed off his rocks. He seemed happy.

Two things happened the next day. One was my mother had to take Fudge to the real barber to do something about his hair. He had plenty left at the back, but just about nothing in front and on top. The barber said there wasn't much he could do until the hair grew back. Between his fangs and his hair he was getting funnier-looking every day.

The second was my father came home with a chain latch for my bedroom door. I could reach it when I stood on tip-toe, but that brother of mine couldn't reach it at all – no matter what!

Our committee was the first to give its report. Mrs Haver said we did a super job. She liked our poster a lot. She thought the silver-sparkle aeroplane was the best. The only thing she asked us was, how come we included a picture of a flying train?

William and the School Report

Richmal Crompton

It was the last day of term. The school had broken up, and William was making his slow and thoughtful way homeward. A casual observer would have thought that William alone among the leaping, hurrying crowd was a true student, that William alone regretted the four weeks of enforced idleness that lay before him. He walked draggingly and as if reluctantly, his brow heavily furrowed, his eyes fixed on the ground. But it was not the thought of the four weeks of holiday that was worrying William. It was a suspicion, amounting almost to a certainty, that he wasn't going to have the four weeks of holiday.

The whole trouble had begun with William's headmaster – a man who was in William's eyes a blend of Nero and Judge Jeffreys and the Spanish Inquisitioners, but who was in reality a harmless inoffensive man, anxious to do his duty to the youth entrusted to his care. William's father had happened to meet him in the train going up to town, and had asked him how William was getting on. The headmaster had replied truthfully and sadly that William didn't seem to be getting on at all. He hadn't, he said, the true scholar's zest for knowledge, his writing was atrocious and he didn't seem able to spell the simplest word or do the simplest sum. Then, brightening, he suggested that William should have coaching during the holidays. Mr Parkinson, one of the Junior form masters who lived near the school, would be at home for the four weeks, and had offered to coach backward boys. An hour a day. It would do William, said the headmaster enthusiastically, all the good in the world. Give him, as it were, an entirely new start. Nothing like individual coaching. Nothing at all. William's father was impressed. He saw four peaceful weeks during which William, daily occupied with his hour of coaching and its complement of homework, would lack both time and spirit to spread around him that devastation that usually marked the weeks of the holiday. He thanked the headmaster profusely, and said that he would let him know definitely later on.

William, on being confronted with the suggestion, was at first speechless with horror. When he found speech it was in the nature of a passionate appeal to all the powers of justice and fair dealing.

"In the *holidays*," he exclaimed wildly. "There's *lors* against it. I'm sure there's *lors* against it. I've never heard of *anyone* having lessons in the holidays. Not *anyone*! I bet even *slaves* didn't have lessons in the holidays. I bet if they knew about it in Parliament, there'd be an inquest about it. Besides I shall only get ill with overworkin' an' get brain fever same as they do in books, an' then you'll have to pay doctors' bills an' p'raps," darkly, "you'll have to pay for my funeral too. I don't see how *anyone* could go on workin' like that for months an' *months* without ever stoppin' once an' not get brain fever and die of it. Anyone'd think you *wanted* me to die. An' if I did die I shun't be surprised if the judge did something to you about it."

His father, unmoved by this dark hint, replied, coolly, "I'm quite willing to risk it."

"An' I don't like Mr Parkinson," went on William gloomily, "he's always cross."

"Perhaps I can arrange it with one of the others," said Mr Brown.

"I don't like any of them," said William, still more gloomily, "they're all always cross."

He contemplated his wrongs in silence for a few minutes, then burst out again passionately:

"'T isn't as if you weren't makin' me pay for that window. It's not fair payin' for it *an'* havin' lessons in the holidays."

141

"It's nothing to do with the window," explained Mr Brown wearily.

"I bet it is," said William darkly. "What else is it if it's not for the window? I've not done anythin' else lately."

"It's because your work at school fails to reach a high scholastic standard," said Mr Brown in a tone of ironical politeness.

"How d'you know?" said William after a moment's thought. "How d'you know it does? You've not seen my report. We don't get 'em till the last day."

"Your headmaster told me so."

"Ole Markie?" said William. "Well," indignantly, "I like that. I *like* that. He doesn't teach me at all. He doesn't teach me anythin' at all. I bet he was jus' makin' it up for somethin' to say to you. He'd got to say somethin' an' he couldn't think of anythin' else to say. I bet he tells everyone he meets that their son isn't doing well at school jus' for somethin' to say. I bet he's got a sort of habit of saying it to everyone he meets an' does it without thinkin'."

"All right," said William's father firmly, "I'll make no arrangements till I've seen your report. If it's a better one than it usually is, of course, you needn't have coaching."

William felt relieved. There were four weeks before the end of the term. Anything might happen. His father might forget about it altogether. Mr Parkinson might develop some infectious disease. It was even possible, though William did not contemplate the possibility with any confidence, that his report might be better. He carefully avoided any reference to the holidays in his father's hearing. He watched Mr Parkinson narrowly for any signs of incipient illness, rejoicing hilariously one morning when Mr Parkinson appeared with what seemed at first to be a rash but turned out on closer inspection to be shaving cuts. He even made spasmodic efforts to display intelligence and interest in class, but his motive in asking questions was misunderstood, and taken to be his usual one of entertaining his friends or holding up the course of the lesson, and he relapsed into his usual state of boredom, lightened by surreptitious games with Ginger.

And now the last day of term had come, and the prospect of holiday coaching loomed ominously ahead. His father had not forgotten. Only last night he had reminded William that it depended on his report whether or not he was to have lessons in the holidays. Mr Parkinson looked almost revoltingly healthy, and in his pocket William carried the worst report he had ever had. Disregarding (in common with the whole school) the headmaster's injunction to give the report to his parents without looking at it first, he had read it apprehensively in the cloakroom and it had justified his blackest fears. He had had wild notions of altering it. The word "poor" could, he thought, easily be changed to "good", but few of the remarks stopped at "poor", and such additions as "Seems to take no interest at all in this subject" and "Work consistently ill prepared" would read rather oddly after the comment "good".

William walked slowly and draggingly. His father would demand the report, and at once make arrangements for the holiday coaching. The four weeks of the holidays stretched – an arid desert – before him.

"But one hour a day can't spoil the whole holidays, William," his mother had said, "you can surely spare one hour out of twelve to improving your mind."

William had retorted that for one thing his mind didn't need improving, and anyway it was *his* mind and he was quite content with it as it was, and for another, one hour a day *could* spoil the whole holidays.

"It can spoil it *absolutely*," he had protested. "It'll just make every single day of it taste of school. I shan't be able to enjoy myself any of the rest of the day after an hour of ole Parkie an' sums an' things. It'll spoil every *minute* of it."

"Well, dear," Mrs Brown had said with a sigh, "I'm sorry, but your father's made up his mind."

William's thoughts turned morosely to that

conversation as he fingered the long envelope in his pocket. There didn't seem to be any escape. If he destroyed the report and pretended that he had lost it, his father would only write to the school for another, and they'd probably make the next one even more damning to pay him out for giving them extra trouble. The only possibility of escape was for him to have some serious illness, and that, William realized gloomily, would be as bad as the coaching.

To make things worse an aunt of his father's (whom William had not seen for several years) was coming over for the day, and William considered that his family was always more difficult to deal with when there were visitors. Having reached the road in which his home was, he halted irresolute. His father was probably coming home for lunch because of the aunt. He might be at home now. The moment when the report should be demanded was, in William's opinion, a moment to be postponed as far as possible. He needn't go home just yet. He turned aside into

146

a wood, and wandered on aimlessly, still sunk in gloomy meditation, dragging his toes in the leaves.

"If ever I get into Parliament," he muttered fiercely, "I'll pass a *lor* against reports."

He turned a bend in the path and came face to face with an old lady. William felt outraged by the sight of her – old ladies had no right to be in the woods – and was about to pass her hurriedly when she accosted him.

"I'm afraid I've lost my way, little boy," she

said breathlessly. "I was directed to take a short cut from the station to the village through the wood, and I think I must have made a mistake."

William looked at her in disgust. She was nearly half a mile from the path that was a short cut from the station to the village.

"What part of the village d'you want to get to?" he said curtly.

"Mr Brown's house," said the old lady, "I'm expected there for lunch."

The horrible truth struck William. This was his father's aunt, who was coming over for the day. He was about to give her hasty directions, and turn to flee from her, when he saw that she was peering at him with an expression of delighted recognition.

"But it's William," she said. "I remember you quite well. I'm your Aunt Augusta. What a good thing I happened to meet you, dear! You can take me home with you."

William was disconcerted for a moment. They were in reality only a very short distance from his home. A path led from the part of the wood where they were across a field to the road where the Browns' house stood. But it was no part of William's plan to return home at once. He'd decided to put off his return as far as possible, and he wasn't going to upset his arrangements for the sake of anyone's aunt, much less his father's.

He considered the matter in frowning silence for a minute, then said:

"All right. You c'n come along with me."

"Thank you, my dear boy," said the old lady brightening. "Thank you. That will be *very* nice. I shall quite enjoy having a little talk with you. It's several years since I met you, but, of course, I recognized you at once."

William shot a suspicious glance at her, but it was evident that she intended no personal insult. She was smiling at him benignly.

She discoursed brightly as William led her further and further into the heart of the wood and away from his home. She told him stories of her far-off childhood, describing in great detail her industry and obedience and perseverance and love of study. She had evidently been a shining example to all her contemporaries.

"There's no joy like the joy of duty done, dear boy," she said. "I'm sure that *you* know that."

"Uh-huh," said William shortly.

As they proceeded on into the wood, however, she grew silent and rather breathless.

"Are we – nearly there, dear boy?" she said.

They had almost reached the end of the wood, and another few minutes would have brought them out into the main road, where a bus would take them to within a few yards of William's home. William still had no intention of going home, and he felt a fierce resentment against his companion. Her chatter had prevented his giving his whole mind to the problem that confronted him. He felt sure that there was a solution if only he could think of it.

He sat down abruptly on a fallen tree and said casually:

"I'm afraid we're lost. We must've took the wrong turning. This wood goes on for miles an' miles. People've sometimes been lost for days."

"With – with no food?" said Aunt Augusta faintly.

"Yes, with no food."

"B-but, they must have died surely?"

"Yes," said William, "quite a lot of 'em were dead when they found 'em."

Aunt Augusta gave a little gasp of terror.

William's heart was less stony than he liked to think. Her terror touched him and he relented.

"Look here," he said, "I think p'raps that path'll get us out. Let's try that path."

"No," she panted. "I'm simply exhausted. I can't walk another step just now. Besides it might only take us further into the heart of the wood."

"Well, I'll go," said William. "I'll go an' see if it leads to the road."

"No, you *certainly* mustn't," said Aunt Augusta sharply, "we must at all costs keep together. You'll miss your way and we shall both be lost separately. I've read of that happening in books. People lost in forests and one going on to find the way and losing the others. No, I'm certainly not going to risk that. I *forbid* you going a yard without me, William, and I'm too much exhausted to walk any more just at present."

William, who had by now tired of the adventure and was anxious to draw it to an end as soon as possible, hesitated, then said vaguely:

"Well . . . s'pose I leave some sort of trail same as they do in books."

"But what can you leave a trail of?" said Aunt Augusta.

Suddenly William's face shone as if illuminated by a light within. He only just prevented himself from turning a somersault into the middle of a blackberry bush.

"I've got an envelope in my pocket," he said. "I'll tear that up. I mean—" he added cryptically, "it's a case of life and death, isn't it?"

"Do be careful then, dear boy," said Aunt Augusta anxiously. "Drop it every *inch* of the way. I hope it's something you can spare, by the way?"

"Oh yes," William assured her, "it's something I can spare all right."

He took the report out of his pocket, and began to tear it into tiny fragments. He walked slowly down the path, dropping the pieces, and taking the precaution of tearing each piece into further fragments as he dropped it. There must be no possibility of its being rescued and put together again. Certain sentences, for instance the one that said, "Uniformly bad. Has made no progress at all", he tore up till the paper on which it was written was almost reduced to its component elements.

The path led, as William had known it would, round a corner and immediately into the main road. He returned a few minutes later, having assumed an expression of intense surprise and delight.

"S'all right," he announced, "the road's jus' round there."

Aunt Augusta took out a handkerchief and

mopped her brow.

"I'm so glad, dear boy," she said. "So very glad. What a relief! I was just wondering how one told edible from inedible berries. We might, as you said, have been here for days ... Now let's just sit here and rest a few minutes before we go home. Is it far by the road?"

"No," said William. "There's a bus that goes all the way."

He took his seat by her on the log, trying to restrain the exuberant expansiveness of his grin. His fingers danced a dance of triumph in his empty pockets.

"I was so much relieved, dear boy," went on Aunt Augusta, "to see you coming back again. It would have been so terrible if we'd lost each other. By the way, what was the paper that you tore up, dear? Nothing important, I hope?"

William had his face well under control by now.

"It was my school report," he said, "I was jus' takin' it home when I met you."

He spoke sorrowfully as one who has lost

his dearest treasure.

Aunt Augusta's face registered blank horror.

"You – you tore up your school report?" she said faintly.

"I had to," said William. "I'd rather," he went on, assuming an expression of noble self-sacrifice, "I'd rather lose my school report than have you starve to death."

It was clear that, though Aunt Augusta was deeply touched by this, her horror still remained.

"But – your school report, dear boy," she said. "It's dreadful to think of your sacrificing that for me. I remember so well the joy and pride of the moment when I handed my school report to my parents. I'm sure you know that moment well."

William, not knowing what else to do, heaved a deep sigh.

"Was it," said Aunt Augusta, still in a tone of deep concern and sympathy, "was it a *specially* good one?"

"We aren't allowed to look at them," said

William unctuously, "they always tell us to take them straight home to our parents without looking at them."

"Of course. Of course," said Aunt Augusta. "Quite right, of course, but – oh, how disappointing for you, dear boy. You have some idea no doubt what sort of report it was?"

"Oh yes," said William, "I've got some sort of an idea all right."

"And I'm sure, dear," said Aunt Augusta, "that it was a very, very good one."

William's expression of complacent modesty was rather convincing.

"Well . . . I – I dunno," he said self-consciously.

"I'm sure it was," said Aunt Augusta. "I know it was. And *you* must know it was really. I can tell that, dear boy, from the way you speak of it."

"Oh . . . I dunno," said William, intensifying the expression of complacent modesty that was being so successful. "I dunno . . ."

"And that tells me that it was," said Aunt

Augusta triumphantly, "far more plainly than if you said it was. I like a boy to be modest about his attainments. I don't like a boy to go about boasting of his successes in school. I'm sure you never do that, do you, dear boy?"

"Oh no," said William with perfect truth. "No, I never do that."

"But I'm so worried about the loss of your report. How quietly and calmly you sacrificed it." It was clear that her appreciation of William's nobility was growing each minute. "Couldn't we try to pick up the bits on our way to the road and piece them together for your dear father to see?"

"Yes," said William. "Yes, we could try'n do that."

He spoke brightly, happy in the consciousness that he had torn up the paper into such small pieces that it couldn't possibly be put together.

"Let's start now, dear, shall we?" said Aunt Augusta. "I'm quite rested."

They went slowly along the little path that

led to the road.

Aunt Augusta picked up the "oo" of "poor" and said, "This must be a 'good' of course," and she picked up the "ex" of "extremely lazy and inattentive" and said, "This must be an 'excellent' of course," but even Aunt Augusta realized that it would be impossible to put together all the pieces.

"I'm afraid it can't be done, dear," she said sadly. "How *disappointing* for you. I feel so sorry that I mentioned it at all. It must have raised your hopes."

"No, it's quite all right," said William, "it's quite all right. I'm not disappointed. Really I'm not."

"I *know* what you're feeling, dear boy," said Aunt Augusta. "I know what I should feel myself in your place. And I hope – I *hope* that I'd have been as brave about it as you are."

William, not knowing what to say, sighed again. He was beginning to find his sigh rather useful. They had reached the road now. A bus was already in sight. Aunt Augusta hailed it, and they boarded it together. They completed the journey to William's house in silence. Once Aunt Augusta gave William's hand a quick surreptitious pressure of sympathy and whispered:

"I know *just* what you are feeling, dear boy."

William, hoping that she didn't, hastily composed his features to their expression of complacent modesty, tinged with deep disappointment – the expression of a boy who has had the misfortune to lose a magnificent school report.

His father was at home, and came to the front door to greet Aunt Augusta.

"Hello!" he said. "Picked up William on the way?"

He spoke without enthusiasm. He wasn't a mercenary man, but this was his only rich unmarried aunt, and he'd hoped that she wouldn't see too much of William on her visit.

Aunt Augusta at once began to pour out a long and confused account of her adventure.

"And we were *completely* lost . . . right in the heart of the wood. I was too much exhausted to go a step farther, but this dear boy went on to explore and, solely on my account because I was nervous of our being separated, he tore up his school report to mark the trail. It was, of course, a great sacrifice for the dear boy, because he was looking forward with such pride and pleasure to watching you read it."

William gazed into the distance as if he saw neither his father nor Aunt Augusta. Only so could he retain his expression of patient suffering.

"Oh, he was, was he?" said Mr Brown sardonically, but in the presence of his aunt forebore to say more.

During lunch, Aunt Augusta, who had completely forgotten her exhaustion and was beginning to enjoy the sensation of having been lost in a wood, enlarged upon the subject of William and the lost report.

"Without a word and solely in order to allay my anxiety, he gave up what I know to be one of the proudest moments one's schooldays have to offer. I'm not one of those people who forget what it is to be a child. I can see myself now handing my report to my mother and father and watching their faces radiant with pride and pleasure as they read it. I'm sure that is a sight that you have often seen, dear boy?"

William, who was finding his expression of virtue hard to sustain under his father's gaze, took refuge in a prolonged fit of coughing which concentrated Aunt Augusta's attention upon him all the more.

"I *do* hope he hasn't caught a cold in that nasty damp wood," she said anxiously. "He took *such* care of me, and I shall never forget the sacrifice he made for me."

"*Was* it a good report, William?" said Mrs Brown with tactless incredulity.

William turned to her an expressionless face.

"We aren't allowed to look at 'em," he said virtuously. "He tells us to bring 'em home without lookin' at 'em."

"But I could tell it was a good report," said Aunt Augusta. "He wouldn't admit it but I could *tell* that he *knew* it was a good report.

He bore it very bravely but I saw what a grief it was to him to have to destroy it—" Suddenly her face beamed. "I know, I've got an idea! Couldn't you write to the headmaster and ask for a duplicate?"

William's face was a classic mask of horror.

"No, don't do that," he pleaded, "don't do that. I-I-I," with a burst of inspiration, "I shun't like to give 'em so much trouble in the holidays."

Aunt Augusta put her hand caressingly on his stubbly head. "*Dear* boy," she said.

William escaped after lunch but, before he joined the Outlaws, he went to the wood and ground firmly into the mud with his heel whatever traces of the torn report could be seen.

It was tea time when he returned. Aunt Augusta had departed. His father was reading a book by the fire. William hovered about uneasily for some minutes.

Then Mr Brown, without raising his eyes from his book, said, "Funny thing, you getting lost in Croome Wood, William. I

should have thought you knew every inch of it. Never been lost in it before, have you?"

"No," said William, and then after a short silence:

"I say . . . Father."

"Yes," said Mr Brown.

"Are you – are you really goin' to write for another report?"

"What sort of a report actually *was* the one you lost?" said Mr Brown, fixing him with a gimlet eye. "Was it a very bad one?"

William bore the gimlet eye rather well.

"We aren't allowed to look at 'em, you know," he said again innocently. "I told you we're told to bring 'em straight home without looking at 'em."

Mr Brown was silent for a minute. As I said before, he wasn't a mercenary man, but he couldn't help being glad of the miraculously good impression that William had made on his only rich unmarried aunt.

"I don't believe," he said slowly, "that there's the slightest atom of doubt, but I'll give you the benefit of it all the same."

William leapt exultantly down the garden and across the fields to meet the Outlaws.

They heard him singing a quarter of a mile away.

Hey, Danny!

Robin Klein

"**R**ight," said Danny's mother sternly. "That schoolbag cost ten dollars. You can just save up your pocket money to buy another one. How could you possibly lose a big schoolbag, anyhow?"

"Dunno," said Danny. "I just bunged in some empty bottles to take back to the milkbar, and I was sort of swinging it round by the handles coming home, and it sort of fell over that culvert thing down on to a truck on the freeway."

"And you forgot to write your name and phone number in it as I told you to," said Mrs Hillerey. "Well, you'll just have to use my blue weekend bag till you save up enough pocket money to replace the old one. And no arguments!"

Danny went and got the blue bag from the hall cupboard and looked at it.

The bag was not just blue; it was a vivid, clear, electric blue, like a flash of lightning. The regulation colour for schoolbags at his school was a khaki-olive-brown, inside and out, which didn't show stains from when your can of Coke leaked, or when you left your salami sandwiches uneaten and forgot about them for a month.

"I can't take this bag to school," said Danny. "Not one this colour. Can't I take my books and stuff in one of those green plastic garbage bags?"

"Certainly not!" said Mrs Hillerey.

On Monday at the bus stop, the kids all stared at the blue bag.

"Hey," said Jim, who was supposed to be his mate. "That looks like one of those bags girls take to ballet classes."

"Hey, Danny, you got one of those frilly dresses in there?" asked Spike.

"Aw, belt up, can't you?" said Danny miserably. On the bus the stirring increased as more and more kids got on. It was a very long trip for Danny. It actually took only twenty minutes – when you had an ordinary brown schoolbag and not a great hunk of sky to carry round with you. Every time anyone spoke to him they called him "Little Boy Blue".

"It matches his lovely blue eyes," said one kid.

"Maybe he's got a little blue trike with training wheels too," said another kid.

"Hey, Danny, why didn't you wear some nice blue ribbons in your hair?"

When Danny got off the bus he made a dash for his classroom and shoved the bag under his desk. First period they had Miss Reynolds, and when she was marking the roll she looked along the aisle and saw Danny's bag and said, "That's a very elegant bag you have there, Danny."

Everyone else looked around and saw the blue bag and began carrying on. Danny kept a dignified silence, and after five minutes Miss Reynolds made them stop singing *A Life on the Ocean Waves*. But all through Maths and English, heads kept turning round to grin at Danny and his radiantly blue bag.

At morning recess he sneaked into the art room and mixed poster paints into a shade of khaki-olive-brown which he rubbed over his bag with his hankie. When the bell rang he had a grey handkerchief, but the bag was still a clear and innocent blue. "Darn thing," Danny muttered in disgust. "Must be made of some kind of special waterproof atomic material. Nothing sticks to it."

"What are you doing in the art room, Daniel?" asked Miss Reynolds. "And what is that terrible painty mess?"

"I was just painting a zodiac sign on my bag," said Danny.

"I wish you boys wouldn't write things all over your good schoolbags. Clean up that mess, Danny, and go to your next class."

But Danny said he was feeling sick and could he please lie down in the sick bay for a while. He sneaked his blue bag in with him, and found the key to the first-aid box and looked inside for something that would turn bright blue bags brown. There was a little bottle of brown lotion, so Danny tipped the whole lot on to cotton wool and scrubbed it into the surface of the bag. But the lotion just ran off the bag and went all over his hands and the bench top in the sick bay.

"Danny Hillerey!" said the school secretary. "You know very well that no student is allowed to unlock the first-aid box. What on earth are you doing?"

"Sorry," said Danny. "Just looking for fruit salts."

"I think you'd better sit quietly out in the fresh air if you feel sick," Mrs Adams said suspiciously. "And who owns that peculiar-looking blue bag?"

"It belongs in the sport equipment shed," said Danny. "It's got measuring tapes and stuff in it. Blue's our house colour."

He went and sat outside with the bag shoved under the seat and looked at it and despaired. Kids from his class started going down to the oval for sport, and someone called out, "It's a beautiful blue, but it hasn't a hood."

Danny glared and said, "Get lost" and, "Drop dead". Then Miss Reynolds came along and made him go down to the oval with the others.

On the way there Danny sloshed the blue bag in a puddle of mud – but nothing happened, the blue became shinier if anything. He also tried grass stains under the sprinkler, which had the same effect. Amongst the line-up of khaki-olive-brown bags, his blue one was as conspicuous as a Clydesdale horse in a herd of small ponies.

"Hey, Danny, what time's your tap dancing lesson?" said the kids.

"Hey, Danny, where did you get that knitting bag? I want to buy one for my aunty."

"Hey, Danny, when did you join the Bluebell marching girls' squad?"

Finally Danny had had enough.

"This bag's very valuable if you want to

know," he said.

"Garn," everyone scoffed. "It's just an ordinary old vinyl bag."

"I had to beg my mum to let me bring that bag to school," said Danny. "It took some doing, I can tell you. Usually she won't let it out of the house."

"Why?" demanded everyone. "What's so special about it?"

Danny grabbed back his bag and wiped off the traces of mud and poster paint and ulcer lotion and grass stains. The bag was stained inside where all that had seeped in through the seams and the zipper, and it would take some explaining when his mother noticed it. (Which she would, next time she went to spend the weekend at Grandma's.) There was her name inside, E. Hillerey, in big neat letters. E for Enid.

"Well," said Danny, "that bag belonged to . . . Well, if you really want to know, it went along on that expedition up Mount Everest."

Everyone jeered.

"It did so," said Danny. "Look, Sir Edmund Hillary, there's his name printed right there inside. And there's a reason it's this funny colour. So it wouldn't get lost in the snow. It was the bag Sir Edmund Hillary carried that flag in they stuck up on top of Mount Everest. But I'm not going to bring it to school any more if all you can do is poke fun at the colour."

Everyone went all quiet and respectful.

"Gee," said Jeff in an awed voice, and he touched the letters that Danny's mother had written with a laundry marking pencil.

"Gosh," said Mark. "We never knew you were related to that Sir Edmund Hillary."

Danny looked modest. "We're only distantly related," he admitted. "He's my dad's second cousin."

"Hey, Danny, can I hold it on the bus? I'll be real careful with it."

"Hey, Danny, can I have a turn when you bring it to school tomorrow?"

"I'll charge you ten cents a go," said Danny. "That's fair, for a bag that went up to the top of Mount Everest."

"Ten cents a kid," he calculated. "One hundred kids at ten cents a turn, ten dollars. A new brown schoolbag. And with a bit of luck, I'll earn all that before someone checks up in the library and finds out Sir Edmund Hillary's name's spelled differently!"

The Mouth-Organ Boys

James Berry

I wanted a mouth-organ, I wanted it more
than anything else in the whole world. I
told my mother. She kept ignoring me, but I
still wanted a mouth-organ badly.

I was only a boy. I didn't have a proper job.
Going to school was like a job, but nobody
paid me to go to school. Again I had to say to
my mother, "Mam, will you please buy a
mouth-organ for me?"

It was the first time, now, that my mother
stood and answered me properly. Yet listen to
what my mother said. "What d'you want a
mouth-organ for?"

"All the other boys have a mouth-organ,
Mam," I told her.

"Why is that so important? You don't have to have something just because others have it."

"They won't have me with them without a mouth-organ, Mam," I said.

"They'll soon change their minds, Delroy."

"They won't, Mam. They really won't. You don't know Wildo Harris. He never changes his mind. And he never lets any other boy change his mind either."

"Delroy, I haven't got the time to argue with you. There's no money to buy a mouth-organ. I bought your new shoes and clothes for Independence celebrations. Remember?"

"Yes, Mam."

"Well, money doesn't come on trees."

"No, Mam." I had to agree.

"It's school-day. The sun won't stand still for you. Go and feed the fowls. Afterwards milk the goat. Then get yourself ready for school."

She sent me off. I had to go and do my morning jobs.

Oh, my mother never listened! She never

understood anything. She always had reasons why she couldn't buy me something and it was no good wanting to talk to my dad. He always cleared off to work early.

All my friends had a mouth-organ, Wildo, Jim, Desmond, Len – everybody had one, except me. I couldn't go round with them now. They wouldn't let anybody go round with them without a mouth-organ. They were now "The Mouth-organ Boys". And we used to be all friends. I used to be their friend. We all used to play games together, and have fun together. Now they pushed me away.

"Delroy! Delroy!" my mother called.

I answered loudly. "Yes, Mam!"

"Why are you taking so long feeding the fowls?"

"Coming, Mam."

"Hurry up, Delroy."

Delroy. Delroy. Always calling Delroy!

I milked the goat. I had breakfast. I quickly brushed my teeth. I washed my face and hands and legs. No time left and my mother said nothing about getting my mouth-organ.

But my mother had time to grab my head and comb and brush my hair. She had time to wipe away toothpaste from my lip with her hand. I had to pull myself away and say, "Good day, Mam."

"Have a good day, Delroy," she said, staring at me.

I ran all the way to school. I ran wondering if the Mouth-organ Boys would let me sit with them today. Yesterday they didn't sit next to me in class.

I was glad the boys came back. We all sat together as usual. But they teased me about not having a mouth-organ.

Our teacher, Mr Goodall, started writing on the blackboard. Everybody was whispering. And it got to everybody talking quite loudly. Mr Goodall could be really cross. Mr Goodall had big muscles. He had a moustache too. I would like to be like Mr Goodall when I grow up. But he could be really cross. Suddenly Mr Goodall turned round and all the talking stopped, except for the voice of Wildo Harris. Mr Goodall held the chalk in his hand and stared at Wildo Harris. He looked at Teacher and dried up. The whole class giggled.

Mr Goodall picked out Wildo Harris for a question. He stayed sitting and answered.

"Will you please stand up when you answer a question?" Mr Goodall said.

Wildo stood up and answered again. Mr Goodall ignored him and asked another question. Nobody answered. Mr Goodall pointed at me and called my name. I didn't know why he picked on me. I didn't know I knew the answer. I wanted to stand up slowly, to kill time. But I was there, standing. I gave an answer.

"That is correct," Mr Goodall said.

I sat down. My forehead felt hot and sweaty, but I felt good. Then in the school yard at recess time, Wildo joked about it. Listen to what he had to say: "Delroy Brown isn't only a big head. Delroy Brown can answer questions with a big mouth."

"Yeah!" the gang roared, to tease me.

Then Wildo had to say, "If only he could get a *mouth*-organ." All the boys laughed and walked away.

I went home to lunch and as usual I came back quickly. Wildo and Jim and Desmond and Len were together, at the bench, under the palm tree. I went up to them. They were swapping mouth-organs, trying out each one. Everybody made sounds on each mouth-organ, and said something. I begged Len, I begged Desmond, I begged Jim, to let me try out their mouth-organs. I only wanted a blow.

They just carried on making silly sounds on each other's mouth-organs. I begged Wildo to lend me his. He didn't even look at me.

I faced Wildo. I said, "Look. I can do something different as a Mouth-organ Boy. Will you let me do something different?"

Boy, everybody was interested. Everybody looked at me.

"What different?" Wildo asked.

"I can play the comb," I said.

"Oh, yeah," Wildo said slowly.

"Want to hear it?" I asked. "My dad taught me how to play it."

"Yeah," Wildo said. "Let's hear it." And not one boy smiled or anything. They just waited.

I took out my comb. I put my piece of tissue-paper over it. I began to blow a tune on my comb and had to stop. The boys were laughing too much. They laughed so much they staggered about. Other children came up and laughed too. It was all silly, laughing at me.

I became angry. Anybody would get mad. I told them they could keep their silly Mouth-

organ Boys business. I told them it only happened because Desmond's granny gave him a mouth-organ for his birthday. And it only caught on because Wildo went and got a mouth-organ too. I didn't sit with the boys in class that afternoon. I didn't care what the boys did.

I went home. I looked after my goats. Then I ate. I told my mum I was going for a walk. I went into the centre of town where I had a great surprise.

The boys were playing mouth-organs and

dancing. They played and danced in the town square. Lots of kids followed the boys and danced around them.

It was great. All four boys had the name "The Mouth-organ Boys" across their chests. It seemed they did the name themselves. They cut out big coloured letters for the words from newspapers and magazines. They gummed the letters down on a strip of brown paper, then they made a hole at each end of the paper. Next a string was pushed through the holes, so they could tie the names round them. The boys looked great. What a super name: "The Mouth-organ Boys"! How could they do it without me!

"Hey, boys!" I shouted, and waved. "Hey, boys!" They saw me. They jumped up more with a bigger act, but ignored me. I couldn't believe Wildo, Jim, Desmond and Len enjoyed themselves so much and didn't care about me.

I was sad, but I didn't follow them. I hung about the garden railings, watching. Suddenly I didn't want to watch any more. I went home slowly. It made me sick how I didn't have a mouth-organ. I didn't want to eat. I didn't want the lemonade and bun my mum gave me. I went to bed.

Mum thought I wasn't well. She came to see me. I didn't want any fussing about. I shut my eyes quickly. She didn't want to disturb me. She left me alone. I opened my eyes again.

If I could drive a truck I could buy loads of mouth-organs. If I was a fisherman I could buy a hundred mouth-organs. If I was an aeroplane pilot I could buy truck-loads of mouth-organs. I was thinking all those things and didn't know when I fell asleep.

Next day at school the Mouth-organ Boys sat with me. I didn't know why but we just sat together and joked a little bit. I felt good running home to lunch in the usual bright sunlight.

I ran back to school. The Mouth-organ Boys were under the palm tree, on the bench. I was really happy. They were really unhappy and cross and this was very strange.

Wildo grabbed me and held me tight. "You thief!" he said.

The other boys came around me. "Let's search him," they said.

"No, no!" I said. "No."

"I've lost my mouth-organ and you have stolen it," Wildo said.

"No," I said. "No."

"What's bulging in your pocket, then?"

"It's mine," I told them. "It's mine."

The boys held me. They took the mouth-organ from my pocket.

"It's mine," I said. But I saw myself up to Headmaster. I saw myself getting caned. I saw myself disgraced.

Wildo held up the mouth-organ. "Isn't this red mouth-organ mine?"

"Of course it is," the boys said.

"It's mine," I said. "I got it at lunch-time."

"Just at the right time, eh?" Desmond said.

"Say you borrowed it," Jim said.

"Say you were going to give it back," Len said.

Oh, I had to get a mouth-organ just when Wildo lost his! "My mother gave it to me at lunch-time," I said.

"Well, come and tell Teacher," Wildo said.

The bell rang. We hurried to our class. My head was aching. My hands were sweating. My mother would have to come to school, and I hated that.

Wildo told our teacher I stole his mouth-organ. It was no good telling Teacher it was mine, but I did. Wildo said his mouth-organ was exactly like that. And I didn't have a mouth-organ.

Mr Goodall went to his desk. And Mr Goodall brought back Wildo's grubby red mouth-organ. He said it was found on the floor.

How could Wildo compare his dirty red mouth-organ with my new, my beautiful, my shining-clean mouth-organ? Mr Goodall made Wildo Harris say he was sorry.

Oh it was good. It was good to become one of "The Mouth-organ Boys".

The Indian in the Cupboard

Lynne Reid Banks

On Omri's birthday, his friend Patrick gives him a plastic Native American Indian, not very exciting. His older brother's present is a small bathroom cupboard, the sort found in old-fashioned bathrooms. When the "plastic" Indian is placed in the cupboard, it becomes real – miniature but alive! His name is Little Bull. Patrick and Omri have a large collection of plastic toys and when Patrick puts a cowboy figure in the cupboard, it too comes to life. His name is Boone. Now there is trouble ahead . . .

Omri slipped his coat on and ran through the bouncing ice-lumps to school. On the way he stopped under a protecting yew tree and took the little men out. He showed them each a large hailstone, which, to them, was the size of a football.

"Now, when we get to school," said Omri, "you must lie very still and quiet in my pockets. I'm putting you in separate ones because I can't risk any fighting or quarrelling. If you're seen I don't know what will happen."

"Danger?" asked Little Bull, his eyes gleaming.

"Yes. Not of death so much. You might be taken away from me. Then you'd never get back to your own time."

"You mean we'd never wake up outta this here drunken dream," said Boone.

But Little Bull was staring at him very thoughtfully. "Own time," he said musingly. "Very strange magic."

Omri had never arrived at school with more apprehension in his heart, not even on spelling-test days. And yet he was excited too. Once he had taken a white mouse to school in his blazer pocket. He'd planned to do all sorts of fiendish things with it, like putting it up his teacher's trouser leg (he had had a man teacher then) or down the back of a girl's neck, or just putting it on the floor and letting it run around and throw the whole class into chaos. (He hadn't actually dared do anything with it except let it peep out and make his neighbours giggle.) This time he had no such plans. All he was hoping was that he could get through the day without anybody finding out what he had in his pockets.

Patrick was waiting for him at the school gate.

"Have you got him?"

"Yes."

His eyes lit up. "Give! I want him."

"All right," said Omri. "But you have to promise that you won't show him to *anybody*."

Omri reached into his right-hand pocket, closed his fingers gently round Boone, and passed him into Patrick's hand.

The moment he'd let go of him, things started to happen.

A particularly nasty little girl called April, who had been playing across the playground at the moment of the transaction, was at Patrick's side about two seconds later.

"What've you got there then, what did he give you?" she asked in her raucous voice like a crow's.

Patrick flushed red. "Nothing! Push off!" he said.

At once April pointed her witchy finger at him. "Look at Patrick blu-shing, look at Patrick blu-shing!" she squawked. Several other children speedily arrived on the scene and soon Patrick and Omri found themselves surrounded.

"What's he got? Bet it's something horrid!"

"Bet it's a slimy toad!"

"A little wriggly worm, more like."

"A beetle!"

"Like him!"

Omri felt his blood begin to get hot in his head. He longed to bash them all one by one, or better still, all at once – Bruce Lee, knocking down hordes of enemies like skittles. He imagined them all rolling backwards down a long wide flight of steps, in waves, bowled over by his flashing fist and flying feet.

The best he could manage in reality, though, was to lower his head and, keeping his hand cupped stiffly over his left pocket, barge through the chanting circle. He caught one of them a good butt in the stomach which was rather satisfying. Patrick was hot on his heels, and they belted across the playground and in through the double doors, which fortunately had just been opened.

Once inside, they were relatively safe. There were teachers all over the place, and any kind of fighting or taunting, above a sly pinch or a snide whisper, was out. Patrick and Omri slowed to a walk, went to their places and sat down, trying to look perfectly calm and ordinary so as not to attract their teacher's attention. Their breathing gave them away, though.

"Well, you two, what are you puffing about? Been running?"

They glanced at each other and nodded.

"So long as you've not been fighting," she said, giving them a sharp look. She always behaved as if a little fight was a long step along the road to hell.

Neither of the boys got much work done during the morning. They couldn't concentrate. Each of them was too aware of the passenger in his pocket. Both Little Bull and Boone were restless, particularly Little Bull. Boone was naturally lazier; he kept dozing off in the dark, and then waking with a little jump that made Patrick very nervous. But Little Bull was scrambling about the whole time.

It was during the third period – when they were all in the main hall listening to the headmaster, whose name was Mr Johnson, announcing plans for the end-of-year show – that Little Bull got really sick and tired of being imprisoned, and started to take drastic action.

The first thing Omri knew was a sharp prick in his hip, as if an insect had stung him. For a moment he was silly enough to think an ant or even a wasp had somehow got into his clothes, and he only just stopped himself from slapping his hand instinctively against his side to squash it. Then there came another jab, sharper than the first, sharp enough in fact to make Omri let out a short yelp.

"Who did that?" asked Mr Johnson irritably.

Omri didn't answer, but the girls sitting near him began giggling and staring.

"Was that you, Omri?"

"Yes. I'm sorry, something stuck into me."

"Patrick! Did you stick a pencil into Omri?" (Such a thing was not unknown during assemblies when they were bored.)

"No, Mr Johnson."

"Well, be quiet when I'm talking!"

Another jab, and this time Little Bull meant business and kept his knife embedded. Omri shouted "Ouch!" and jumped to his feet.

"Omri! Patrick! Leave the hall!"

"But I didn't—" began Patrick.

"Out, I said!" shouted Mr Johnson furiously.

They left, Patrick walking normally and Omri dancing about like a flea on a hot stove, shouting "Ow! OW!" at every step as Little Bull continued to dig the needle-point of his knife in. The whole school was in hysterics of laughter (and Mr Johnson was frothing with rage) by the time they reached the swing-doors and departed.

Outside, they ran (well, Patrick ran and Omri performed a series of sideways leaps) to the far end of the playground. On the way Omri plunged his hand into his pocket, seized Little Bull, and dragged him out. The agony stopped.

Safe in a sheltered corner behind some privet bushes Omri held his persecutor at eye-level and shook him violently, the way you shake a bottle of medicine. He called him the worst names he could possibly think of. When he'd run out of swear-words (which was not for some time) he hissed, like Mr Johnson, "What do you mean by it? How dare you? How dare you stick your knife into me?"

"Little Bull dare! Omri keep in dark many hours! Little Bull want to see school place, not lie in hot dark! No breathe, no see! Want *enjoy*!"

"I warned you you wouldn't, it's not my fault you made me bring you! Now you've got me into trouble."

Little Bull looked mulish, but he stopped shouting. Seeing this evidence that a truce was on its way, Omri calmed down a bit too.

"Listen. I can't let you see because I can't take you out. You have no idea what would happen if I did. If any of the other children saw you they'd want to grab you and mess you about – you'd hate it, and it would be terribly dangerous too, you'd probably get hurt or killed. You've *got* to lie quiet till school's over. I'm sorry if you're bored but it's your own fault."

Little Bull thought this over and then he said a most astonishing thing.

"Want Boone."

"What? Your enemy?"

"Better enemy than alone in dark."

Patrick had taken Boone out of his pocket. The little cowboy was sitting on his hand. They were gazing at each other. Omri said, "Boone, Little Bull says he wants you. He's lonely and bored."

"Well, ain't that jest too bad!" said Boone sarcastically. "After he tried to kill me, now he's come over all lovey-dovey. Listen, you redskin!" he shouted through cupped hands across the yawning gulf between Patrick and Omri. "I don't care how lonesome y'are! Ah don't care if'n ya drop down daid! Th'only good Injun's a daid Injun, d'ya hear me?"

Little Bull turned his head haughtily away.

"I think he's lonely too, really," said Patrick in a whisper. "He's been crying."

"Oh no, not again!" said Omri. "Honestly, Boone – at your age—"

Just then they heard their teacher calling them from the school door.

"Come on, you two! You've not got the day off, you know!"

"Give me your knife," said Omri to Little Bull on a sudden impulse. "Then I'll put you together." With only a moment's hesitation, Little Bull handed over his knife. Omri slipped it into the small breast-pocket of his shirt which was empty and where it wouldn't easily get lost. Then he said to Patrick, "Let me have Boone."

"No!"

"Just for the next lesson. Then at lunch time you can have both of them. They'll keep each other company. They can't do each other much damage in a pocket."

Reluctantly Patrick handed Boone over. Omri held them one in each hand so they were face to face.

"Be good, you two. Try talking to each other instead of fighting. But whatever you do, don't make any noise." And he slipped them both into his left-hand pocket and he and Patrick ran back to the school buildings.

What was left of the morning passed uneventfully. Omri even got a few sums done. By the time the first whiffs of school dinner were beginning to flood through the classrooms, Omri was congratulating himself on a stroke of genius in putting the two little men together. There had not been another peep out of either of them, and when Omri took an opportunity (when the teacher's back was turned) to open his pocket stealthily and peer down into it, he was pleased to see them, sitting in the bottom of it, face to face, apparently having a conversation. They were both gesticulating with their arms – there was too much noise all round for Omri to be able to hear their tiny voices.

He had given some thought to the matter of their dinner. He would separate them for that, one into each pocket and slip some dry bits of food down to them. Omri let himself play with the wonderful fantasy of what the other kids' reaction would be if he casually brought them out and sat them on the edge of his plate . . . Funny to think that he would certainly have done it, only a week ago, without thinking about the dangers.

The bell rang at last. There was the usual stampede, and Omri found himself in the queue next to Patrick.

"Come on, then, hand them over," Patrick whispered over his tray as they shuffled towards the fragrant hatches.

"Not *now*, everyone'd see."

"You said at lunchtime."

"After lunch."

"Now. I want to feed them."

"Well, you can have Boone, but I want to

198

feed Little Bull."

"You said I could have them both!" said Patrick, no longer in a whisper. Others in the queue began to turn their heads.

"Will you shut up?" hissed Omri.

"No," said Patrick in a loud clear voice. He held out his hand.

Omri felt trapped and furious. He looked into Patrick's eyes and saw what happens even to the nicest people when they want something badly and are determined to get it, come what may. Omri slammed his empty tray down on the floor and, taking Patrick by the wrist, pulled him out of the queue and into a quiet corner of the hall.

"Listen to me," he grated out between teeth clenched in anger. "If you let anything happen to Little Bull, I will bash you so hard your teeth will fall out." (This, of course, is the sort of thing that happens even to the nicest people when they are in a trap.) With that, he groped in his pocket and brought the two little men out. He didn't look at them or say goodbye to them. He just put them carefully into Patrick's hand and walked away.

He had lost his appetite, so he didn't get back in the queue; but Patrick did. He even pushed a bit, he was so eager to get some food to give to the cowboy and the Indian. Omri watched from a distance. He wished now he hadn't been too angry to give Patrick some pretty clear instructions. Like telling him to separate them. Now he thought about it, perhaps it wasn't a good idea to feed them in a pocket. Who wants to eat something that's descended between two layers of cloth and collected bits of dust and fluff! If he'd still had them, he would have taken them to some private place and taken them out to eat properly. Why had he ever brought them to school at all? The dangers here were too awful.

Watching, he suddenly stiffened. Patrick had reached the hatch now and received his dinner. He almost ran with it to a table – he did try to go to one in the outside row near the windows, but a dinner-lady stopped him and made him sit in the middle of the hall. There were children all round him and on either side. Surely, thought Omri, surely he wasn't going to try to feed them there?

He saw Patrick take a pinch of bread and slip it into his pocket. He wasn't wearing a jacket; the men were in his jeans pocket. Fortunately the jeans were new and loose, but still he had to half stand up to get the bit of bread in; when he was sitting down the people in his pocket must be pretty well squashed against his leg. Omri imagined them trying to eat, held down flat by two thick layers of cloth. He could almost see Patrick imagining it too. He was frowning uneasily and shifting around in his chair. The girl next to him spoke to him. She was probably telling him not to wriggle. Patrick said something sharp in reply. Omri sucked in his breath. If only Patrick wouldn't draw attention to himself!

Suddenly he gasped. The girl had given Patrick a hard push. He pushed her back. She nearly went off her chair. She stood up and pushed him with all her might, using both hands. He went flying over backwards, half on to the boy on the other side of him, who jumped from his place, spilling part of his dinner. Patrick landed on the floor.

Omri didn't stop to think. He raced towards him across the hall, dodging in and out among the tables. His heart was hammering with terror. If Patrick had fallen on them! Omri had a terrible, fleeting vision of the pocket of Patrick's jeans, with bloodstains spreading – he clamped down on his imagination.

By the time he got there, Patrick was back on his feet, but now the other boy was angry and clearly looking for a fight. The girl on his other side looked ready to clobber him too. Omri pushed between them, but a stout dinner-lady was ahead of him.

"'Ere, 'ere, what's goin' on?" she asked, barging in with her big stomach and sturdy arms. She grabbed Patrick in one hand and the boy with the other and kind of dangled them at arm's length and shook them. "No fightin' in 'ere, thank you very much, or it'll be off to the 'ead master's orfice before you can say knife, the 'ole bloomin' pack of you!" She dumped them down in their separate chairs as if they'd been bags of shopping. They were both thoroughly tousled and red-faced. Omri's eyes shot down to Patrick's thigh. No blood. No movement either, but at least no blood.

Everyone began to eat again as the stout

dinner-lady stamped away, tut-tutting as she went. Omri leant over the back of Patrick's chair and whispered out of a dry mouth, "Are they all right?"

"How do I know," said Patrick sulkily. But his hand crept down and delicately explored the slight bump on the top of his leg where his pocket was. Omri held his breath. "Yeah, they're OK. They're moving," he muttered.

Omri went out into the playground. He felt too jumpy to stay indoors, or eat, or anything. How would he get them back from Patrick, who, quite obviously, was not a fit person to have charge of them? Nice as he was, as a friend, he just wasn't fit. It must be because he didn't take them seriously yet. He simply didn't seem to realize that they were *people*.

When the bell rang Omri still hadn't come to any decision. He hurried back into school. Patrick was nowhere to be seen. Omri looked round for him frantically. Maybe he'd gone into the washroom to be private and give the men something to eat. Omri went in there and called him softly, but there was no answer. He returned to his place in the classroom. There was no sign of Patrick. And there was no further sign of him till about halfway through the lesson – not one word of which Omri took in, he was so worried.

At last, when the teacher turned her back to write on the board, Patrick slipped round a partition, rushed across the room silently and dropped into his chair.

"Where the *heck* have you been?" asked Omri under his breath.

"In the music-room," said Patrick smugly. The music-room was not a room at all, but a little alcove off the gym in which the musical instruments were stored, together with some of the bulkier apparatus like the jumping horse. "I sat under the horse and fed them," he muttered out of the side of his mouth. "Only they weren't very hungry."

"I bet they weren't!" said Omri, "after all they'd been through!"

"Cowboys and Indians are used to rough treatment," Patrick retorted. "Anyway, I left some food in my pocket for later if they want it."

"It'll get all squashy."

"Oh, so what? Don't fuss so much, they don't mind!"

"How do you know what they mind?" said Omri hotly, forgetting to whisper. The teacher turned round.

"Oh ho, so there you are, Patrick! And where have you been, may I enquire?"

"Sorry, Miss Hilton."

"I didn't ask if you were sorry. I asked where you'd been."

Patrick coughed and lowered his head. "In the wash-room," he mumbled.

"For nearly twenty minutes? I don't believe you! Are you telling me the truth?" Patrick mumbled something. "Patrick, answer me. Or I'll send you to the headmaster."

This was the ultimate threat. The headmaster was very fierce and could make you feel five centimetres high. So Patrick said, "I was in the music-room, and that's true. And I forgot the time."

And that's not true, added Omri silently. Miss Hilton was nobody's fool. She knew it too.

"You'd better go and see Mr Johnson," she said. "Omri, you go too, chattering away there as usual. Tell him I said you were both disturbing the class and that I'm tired of it."

They got up silently and walked through the tables, while all the girls giggled and the boys smirked or looked sorry for them, according to whether they liked them or not. Omri glanced at Patrick under his eyebrows. They were for it now.

Outside the headmaster's office they stopped.

"You knock," whispered Omri.

"No, you," retorted Patrick.

They dithered about for a few minutes, but it was useless to put it off, so in the end they both knocked together.

"Yes?" came a rather irritable voice from inside.

They edged round the door. Mr Johnson

was seated at his large desk, working at some papers. He looked up at once.

"Well, you two? What was it this time – fighting in the playground or talking in class?"

"Talking," they said, and Patrick added, "And I was late."

"Why?"

"I just was."

"Oh, don't waste my time!" snapped Mr Johnson. "There must have been a reason."

"I was in the music-room, and I forgot the time," Patrick repeated.

"I don't remember you being especially musical. What were you doing in the music-room?"

"Playing."

"Which instrument?" asked Mr Johnson with a touch of sarcasm.

"Just – playing."

"*With what?*" he asked, raising his voice.

"With a – with—" he glanced at Omri. Omri threw him a warning grimace.

"What are you pulling faces about, Omri?

You look as if someone's just stuck a knife into you."

Omri started to giggle, and that set Patrick off.

"Somebody just did!" spluttered Patrick.

Mr Johnson was in no such jolly mood, however. He was scowling horribly.

"What are you talking about, you silly boy? Stop that idiotic noise!"

Patrick's giggles were getting worse. If they hadn't been where they were, Omri thought, Patrick would have folded up completely.

"Someone – did – stick a knife into him!" hiccupped Patrick, and added, "A very small one!" His voice went off into a sort of whinny.

Omri had stopped giggling and was staring in awful anticipation at Patrick. When Patrick got into this state he was apt to do and say anything, like someone who's drunk. He took hold of his arm and gave it a sharp shake.

"Shut up!" he hissed.

Mr Johnson got up slowly and came round his desk. Both boys fell back a step, but

Patrick didn't stop giggling. On the contrary, it got worse. He seemed to be getting completely helpless. Mr Johnson loomed over him and took him by the shoulder.

"Listen here, my lad," he said in fearsome tones. "I want you to pull yourself together this moment and tell me what you meant. If there is any child in this school who so far forgets himself as to stick knives into people, or even pretend to, I want to know about it! Now, who was it?"

"Little – Bull!" Patrick squeaked out. Tears were running down his cheeks.

Omri gasped. "Don't!"

"Who?" asked Mr Johnson, puzzled.

Patrick didn't answer. He couldn't. He was now speechless with nervous, almost hysterical laughter.

Mr Johnson gave him a shake of his own that rocked him back and forth on his feet like one of those weighted dolls that won't fall down. Then, abruptly, he let him go and strode back to his desk.

"You seem to be quite beyond yourself," he

said sharply. "I think the only thing I can do is telephone your father."

Patrick stopped laughing instantly.

"Ah, that's better!" said Mr Johnson. "Now. Who did you say had stabbed Omri?"

Patrick stood rigid, like a soldier at attention. He didn't look at Omri, he just stared straight at Mr Johnson.

"I want the truth, Patrick, and I want it now!"

"Little Bull," said Patrick very clearly and much louder than necessary.

"Little Who?"

"Bull."

Mr Johnson looked blank, as well he might. "Is that somebody's nickname, or is this your idea of a joke?"

Patrick gave his head one stiff shake. Omri was staring at him, as if paralysed. Was he going to tell? He knew Patrick was afraid of his father.

"Patrick. I shall ask you once more. Who is this – Little Bull?"

Patrick opened his mouth. Omri clenched

his teeth. He was helpless. Patrick said, "He's an Indian."

"A what?" asked Mr Johnson. His voice was very quiet now. He didn't sound annoyed any more.

"An Indian."

Mr Johnson looked at him steadily for some seconds, his chin resting on his hand.

"You are too old to tell those sort of lies," he said quietly.

"It's not a lie!" Patrick shouted suddenly, making both Omri and Mr Johnson jump. "It's not a lie! He's a real live Indian!"

To Omri's utter horror, he saw that Patrick was beginning to cry. Mr Johnson saw it too. He was not an unkind man. No headmaster is much good if he can't scare the wits out of children when necessary, but Mr Johnson didn't enjoy making them cry.

"Now then, Patrick, none of that," he said gruffly. But Patrick misunderstood. He thought he was still saying he didn't believe him.

He now said the words Omri had been

dreading most.

"It's true and I can prove it!"

And his hand went to his pocket.

Omri did the only thing possible. He jumped at him and knocked him over. He sat on his chest and pinned his hands to the ground.

"You dare – you dare – you dare—" he ground out between clenched teeth before Mr Johnson managed to drag him off.

"Get out of the room!" he roared.

"I won't!" Omri choked out. He'd be crying himself in a minute, he felt so desperate.

"OUT!"

Omri felt his collar seized. He was almost hiked off his feet. The next thing he knew, he was outside the door and hearing the key turning.

Without stopping to think, Omri hurled himself against the door, kicking and banging with his fists.

"Don't show him, Patrick, don't show him! Patrick, don't, I'll kill you if you show him!" he screamed at the top of his lungs.

Footsteps came running. Through his tears and a sort of red haze, Omri just about saw Mrs Hunt, the headmaster's elderly secretary, bearing down on him. He got in a couple more good kicks and shouts before she had hold of him and, with both arms round his waist, carried him, shrieking and struggling, bodily into her own little office.

The minute she put him down he tried to bolt, but she hung on.

"Omri! Omri! Stop it, calm down, whatever's come over you, you naughty boy!"

"Please don't let him! Go in and stop him!" Omri cried.

"Who? What?"

Before Omri could explain he heard the sound of footsteps from the next room. Suddenly Mr Johnson appeared, holding Patrick by the elbow. The headmaster's face was dead white, and his mouth was partly open. Patrick's head was hung down and his shoulders were heaving with sobs. One look at him told Omri the worst. Patrick had shown the headmaster.

Friday

Susan Cooper

The air-raid siren went at the beginning of the afternoon, in an English lesson, while Mrs Wilson was reading them *Children of the New Forest*. At first they couldn't hear the siren at all for the school whistles: a chorus of alarm, their own indoor warning, shrilling down all the corridors at once.

"Ma'am, ma'am! A raid, ma'am!"

Mrs Wilson closed the book with a deliberate snap and stood up. "All right now, children, quickly and quietly. Books in your desks, take out your gas masks, all stand up. Anybody not got his gas mask? Very good. Now I want a nice neat line to the shelter, and no running."

A hand was waving wildly at the front of the class. "Ma'am, is it a real raid, ma'am?"

"It's a drill," said a scornful voice.

"It's the wrong time for a drill."

Mrs Wilson scowled, and they knew the scowl and were quiet. "We don't know yet. Door monitor?"

Little Albert Russell was already stiff at attention by the open door, the strap of his gas mask case neat across his chest. Out they went into the corridor, from one row of desks at a time, their double file jostling the filing classes from the other rooms, out to the air-raid shelters in the playground.

Derek and Peter had desks near the classroom window. Geoffrey was behind them.

"Can you see anything?"

"Nah. Hear the siren now, though. Listen."

The head-splitting school whistles had stopped, and Derek listened as he walked, and heard the distant wail of the siren rise and fall until they were down the corridor and going out of the big double door. He and

Peter and Geoff were nearly at the end of the line; Mrs Wilson was counting heads just in front of them. He shivered; the sun was shining through broken clouds, but there was a chill wind. Most of the other classes, the younger ones, were made to take their overcoats into the shelters, but his group, the farthest from the cloakrooms, had no time ever to fetch theirs.

He became conscious suddenly of the drone of engines somewhere high up.

"Look!" Peter stopped, excited, pointing.

The three couples behind them fell over their feet as he stopped, and then skirted him and went nervously, disapprovingly on. Only Geoffrey paused. The girl who had been walking with him called over her shoulder, "Come *on*," but she was Susan Simmons, who was always bossy, and the boys took no notice, but stood where they were and stared up.

Where Peter was pointing, there was a pattern of slow-moving dots in the sky. The deep hum of the engines grew as he watched, and developed a kind of throbbing sound.

217

The clouds were very high, and the planes were flying below them; they seemed light-coloured and were not easy to see unless the sun went behind a cloud. Their noise seemed so loud now that Derek looked all around the rest of the sky for more, but saw nothing except the familiar floating shapes of the seven barrage balloons, three near, four far off, fat silver ovals hanging up there with bulbous fins at their tails, like great friendly bloated fish. The balloons were filled with hydrogen, he knew, and tethered by thick cables; they were there to get in the way of any Nazi pilot coming in low to drop his bombs.

"Junkers," Geoffrey said confidently. "Junker eighty-eights."

What with his own excitement and the height of the formation, Derek could not really make out the silhouette of any individual plane; but by the same token he knew that Geoff couldn't either. "No, no," he said. "Dorniers."

And then in the second that they still

paused on the black asphalt playground, with the grubby concrete boxes that were the air-raid shelters looming ahead of them, they saw the unbelievable happen. Suddenly, the rigid, steadily advancing formation of enemy planes broke its pattern, lost its head as plane after plane broke away and dived; and they heard a new higher noise and glimpsed, diving through a broad gap in the clouds out of the sun, a gaggle of other smaller planes scattering the bombers as a dog scatters sheep. It was a furious sky now, full of coughing gunfire.

They heard other guns open up, deeper, closer, on the ground.

"Gosh!" Derek said. He had forgotten entirely where he was; he hopped in delight. His gas mask case banged at his back. "*Gosh!*"

"Fighters, our fighters!" Peter waved madly at the sky. "Look!"

And they were lost in breathless looking and in the growing scream of engines and the thumping of gunfire, as an urgent hand came

down and Mrs Wilson dragged them off towards the shelter.

"You *stupid* boys, come under cover *at once!*" Her voice was a squeak of anxious rage, and it was only the realization that she was angrier than they had ever seen her that brought them skidding into the entrance to the shelter. But even then Peter was still staring back over his shoulder, and all at once he let out a yell of such joyful surprise that all four of them, even Mrs Wilson, paused, hypnotized, for a last glimpse of the sky.

"He's got him, he's got him, he's got him!"

It was a Hurricane – Derek could see the blunt nose now – and it had dived after one of the weaving bombers, with its guns making bright flashes on its wings. And the bomber had been hit: it was trailing a ragged path of black smoke behind it and lurching erratically across the sky and down. It was still firing its guns; you could hear them and see them among the puffs of smoke in the sky that were the bursts of shells fired from the ground. Nearer and nearer the ground the plane came, a long way away from them but still visible, and as it dived, it veered close to one of the motionless silver barrage balloons, and suddenly there was a sound like a soft "whoomph" and a great burst of flame.

The plane dropped and vanished, with the victorious Hurricane above it swooping off to join the battle that they could still hear but no longer see; the sound of the crash was no more than a faraway thump, like the firing of one of the anti-aircraft guns, but enough to galvanize Mrs Wilson into thrusting them ahead of her around the right-angle bend of the entrance into the shelter itself. But still Derek had one moment's last quick sight over his shoulder of the burning barrage balloon, hanging there in the sky as it always had but beginning strangely to droop, with its flat inflated fins no longer sticking firmly out but curving gently, wearily, down.

When they came out of the shelter about half an hour later, the barrage balloon was no longer there. Instead, there was a gap in the sky and only six floating guardian shapes. The raid had not lasted for very long; there had been time for a handful of songs – the other three classes of children in their shelters had been singing "Waltzing Matilda" when they came in – and the distribution of one boiled sweet each. Then the noise outside, which they heard only in the brief gap between one song and the next, had died away, and the long single note of the "all clear" had shrilled out. They went back to their classrooms, in as neat a double file as before, and bossy Susan Simmons made a shocked face at Derek and Peter and Geoff and whispered to her friends as they passed.

The three boys stayed after school, hovering at their desks until everyone else had left, to apologize to Mrs Wilson, and curiously she did no more than give them a brief lecture on the perils of being out in the open when a raid was on, and the undeniable extra crime of giving someone else the risk of coming to haul them inside.

"She's nice," Derek said on the way home. "I mean, she could have sent us to the Head, and then they'd have told our parents, and there'd have been an awful row."

"She ought to be grateful, if you ask me," Peter said. "If she hadn't had to come and find us, she'd have missed all the fun."

ACKNOWLEDGEMENTS

The publishers wish to thank the following for permission to use copyright material:

Lynne Reid Banks: for material from *An Indian in the Cupboard*, first published by J.M. Dent & Sons Ltd (1981) pp. 132–53, reproduced by permission of Watson, Little Ltd on behalf of the author.

Steve Barlow and Steve Skidmore: for material from *Vernon Bright and the Magnetic Banana*, pp. 1–9, first published by Puffin (2000). Copyright © Steve Barlow and Steve Skidmore, 2000, reproduced by permission of Penguin Books Ltd.

Judy Blume: for "The Flying Train Committee" from *Tales of a Fourth Grade Nothing* by Judy Blume, published by Bodley Head (1979). Copyright © 1972 by Judy Blume, reproduced by permission of The Random House Group Ltd and Dutton Children's Books, an imprint of Penguin Putnam Books for Young Readers, a division of Penguin Putnam, Inc.

Susan Cooper: for "Friday" from *Dawn of Fear* by Susan Cooper, first published by Bodley Head. Copyright © 1970 by Susan Cooper Grant, reproduced by permission of The Random House Group Ltd and Harcourt, Inc.

Gillan Cross: for "The Ruined Minibus" and "Barny's Idea" from *Swimathon!* by Gillian Cross, first published by Methuen Children's Books Ltd (1986), reissued by Mammoth, an imprint of Egmont Children's Books Ltd (1998). Copyright © 1986 Gillian Cross, reproduced by permission of Egmont UK and the author.

Robyn Klein: for "Hey, Danny" from *Ratbags and Rascals* by Robyn Klein, first published by Jacaranda Wiley (1984). Copyright © 1984 Robin Klein, reproduced by permission of Curtis Brown (Aust) Pty Ltd, Sydney, on behalf of the author.

George Layton: for "The Christmas Party" from *The Fib and Other Stories* by George Layton, first published by Longman (1978). Copyright © 1978 George Layton, reproduced by permission of Pearson Education Ltd.

Rob Marsh: for "The Boy Who Could Tell the Future" from *Tales of Mystery and Suspense* by Rob Marsh, first published by Struik Publishers (Pty) Ltd (1994), reproduced by permission of Struik Publishers (Pty) Ltd.

Laura Ingalls Wilder: for "School" from *On the Banks of Plum Creek* by Laura

ACKNOWLEDGEMENTS

Ingalls Wilder, first published by Methuen & Co Ltd (1958), reprinted by
Mammoth, an imprint of Egmont Children's Books Ltd. Copyright © 1937 by
Laura Ingalls Wilder, renewed 1965 by Roger L. Macbride, reproduced by
permission of Egmont UK.

Every effort has been made to trace the copyright holders but where this has
not been possible or where any error has been made the publishers will be
pleased to make the necessary arrangement at the first opportunity.

More top stories can be found in

Scary Stories for Eight Year Olds

Chosen by Helen Paiba

Spine-chilling stories include:

The Ghost of Old Man Chompers

The Bones That Came Back to Life

The Blood-thirsty Crocodile

The Girl Who Ate Too Much Chocolate

The Ghost Dog's Revenge

More top stories can be found in

Funny Stories
for Eight Year Olds

Chosen by Helen Paiba

Hilarious stories include:

The Unidentified Flying Dog

The Man Who Couldn't Stop Laughing

The Amazing Talking Baby

The Boy Who Turned into a Frog

The Exploding Jelly Custard Surprise

More top stories can be found in

Adventure Stories
for Eight Year Olds

Chosen by Helen Paiba

Action-packed stories include:

Horror on a Haunted Boat

The Fearsome Flying Princess

Adventure in the Wild West!

The Chicken-pox Treasure Hunt

An Amazing Ascape from Kidnap

More top stories can be found in

Revolting Stories for Nine Year Olds

Chosen by Helen Paiba

Disgusting stories include:

The Curse of the Lingering Stink

Tourists for Tea . . .

The Repulsive Revenge of the Headless Chicken

The Truth of the Snotty Snail Trail

Books in this series available from Macmillan

The prices shown below are correct at the time of going to press.
However, Macmillan Publishers reserves the right to show new retail
prices on covers which may differ from those previously advertised.

Adventure Stories for Five Year Olds	0 330 39137 2	£4.99
Animal Stories for Five Year Olds	0 330 39125 9	£4.99
Bedtime Stories for Five Year Olds	0 330 48366 8	£4.99
Funny Stories for Five Year Olds	0 330 39124 0	£4.99
Magical Stories for Five Year Olds	0 330 39122 4	£4.99
Adventure Stories for Six Year Olds	0 330 39138 0	£4.99
Animal Stories for Six Year Olds	0 330 36859 1	£4.99
Bedtime Stories for Six Year Olds	0 330 48368 4	£4.99
Funny Stories for Six Year Olds	0 330 36857 5	£4.99
Magical Stories for Six Year Olds	0 330 36858 3	£4.99
Adventure Stories for Seven Year Olds	0 330 39139 9	£4.99
Animal Stories for Seven Year Olds	0 330 35494 9	£4.99
Funny Stories for Seven Year Olds	0 330 34945 7	£4.99
Scary Stories for Seven Year Olds	0 330 34943 0	£4.99
School Stories for Seven Year Olds	0 330 48378 1	£4.99
Adventure Stories for Eight Year Olds	0 330 39140 2	£4.99
Animal Stories for Eight Year Olds	0 330 35495 7	£4.99
Funny Stories for Eight Year Olds	0 330 34946 5	£4.99
Scary Stories for Eight Year Olds	0 330 34944 9	£4.99
School Stories for Eight Year Olds	0 330 48379 X	£4.99
Adventure Stories for Nine Year Olds	0 330 39141 0	£4.99
Animal Stories for Nine Year Olds	0 330 37493 1	£4.99
Funny Stories for Nine Year Olds	0 330 37491 5	£4.99
Revolting Stories for Nine Year Olds	0 330 48370 6	£4.99
Scary Stories for Nine Year Olds	0 330 37492 3	£4.99
Adventure Stories for Ten Year Olds	0 330 39142 9	£4.99
Animal Stories for Ten Year Olds	0 330 39128 3	£4.99
Funny Stories for Ten Year Olds	0 330 39127 5	£4.99
Revolting Stories for Ten Year Olds	0 330 48372 2	£4.99
Scary Stories for Ten Year Olds	0 330 39126 7	£4.99

All Pan Macmillan titles can be ordered from our website,
www.panmacmillan.com, or from your local bookshop
and are also available by post from:

Bookpost
PO Box 29, Douglas, Isle of Man IM99 1BQ

Credit cards accepted. For details:
Telephone: +44(0)1624 677237
Fax: +44(0)1624 670923
Email: bookshop@enterprise.net
www.bookpost.co.uk

Free postage and packing in the UK.